I Don't Really Get Jan-Andrew Henderson

Jan-Andrew Henderson

Black Hart
Edinburgh. Brisbane.

First published 2020 by Black Hart

Black Hart Entertainment.
Blackhartentertainment.com

Cover by Panagiotis Lampridis (BookDesignStars)
Book Layout © 2017 BookDesignTemplates.com

I Don't Really Get
ISBN 978-1-63625-858-4
ISBN 978-1-63625-840-9 eBook

The Stories

Praise for Jan-Andrew Henderson

'One of the UK's most promising writers'
Edinburgh Evening News

'One of the UK's best talents'
Lovereading.co.uk

'Jan Henderson writes the kind of thrillers that make
you miss your stop on the bus'
Times Educational Supplement

'A moving, funny and original writer'
The Austin Chronicle

'Jan Henderson has written some incredible books...
One of my favourite authors'
Sharon Rooney (*My Mad Fat Diary. The Electrical
Life of Louis Wain. Barbie*)

'If there were more books like yours out there, maybe
people would be reading more'
Charlie Higson (*Young James Bond* and *The Enemy*
series)

One of the symptoms of an approaching nervous breakdown is the belief that one's work is terribly important.

Bertrand Russell. *The Conquest of Happiness.*

For Siobhan

Chocolate Drops

Ma faither killed ma sister.

Twice.

Then he battered 6-inch nails intae her coffin wi his bare, mucky, scabby auld plumber's hauns an danced the Dashin White Sergeant on her grave, while his beardie, drunken, bent-nosed cronies sang 'Donald Whuar's yer Troosers' an pissed against the cemetery wall.

Me? I held the hammer.

Mah sister's name wis Minty Broon - I gave her that nickname cause o this greeny tinge she hid roond aboot her teeth. No rotten or nothin - just the way they looked. An she had this antiseptic smell, a wee bit like washin up liquid. Her friends didnae notice I suppose - abody thought she wis dead bonny But it's different when someone's yir sister, an you see them evolve, if ye ken whit I mean… an that's no always sae pretty. I think that beauty works better if it jumps oot an slaps you in the puss. Aye, an how it works in reverse is interestin an all - so's you can still love the wife, even after she's turned intae a fat, ugly beezer.

Mah faither's Big Don. Minty was the apple in his eye, but that fat shite woulnae've noticed the milk in his cornflakes goin aff. Ach... he wis a day-tae-day man. Called Minty 'Chocolate Broon'. He just changed mah nickname cause he wasnae smart enough tae think up one of his own - and it didnae even make sense.

Minty. Minty aye looked awfy nice, wi her long black dresses an her short, black hair. Confident, an aw the guys went after her, cause she didnae pay nae mind tae them. I wondered aboot that at the time - bein jist a young loon, I suppose. I dinnae ken.

I'd watch in clubs, how the girls seem to a fancy the guy whit looks like he's no bothered. Seems he's havin a fine time wi hissel, an that makes aw the girls think they'd hae a fine time wi him too. Good, eh?

I copied that, an guess what?

Sometimes it worked an sometimes no.

It's not like I didnae hae a few wee talents o my own. I wis good in bed. There's nae point denying it. So I wisnae short of a bit o muff. Aye... I had an artistic turn of phrase, an aw. Thought aboot mebee bein a writer.

So I wisnae too bothered aboot stuff, an I wisnae bothered when Minty wis. Aye? I cannae really describe it.

See... she didnae listen tae the news wi hauf an ear like me - or treat it like anither type o Saturday night TV entertainment, like Big Don. I dinnae suppose she could talk tae us. I dinnae ken. Our mum had left donkeys ago an Minty's girlfriends were goldfish wi tits, if ye ken whit I mean. Aw the boys just wanted tae shag her. It wis a wee toon.

The smart folk she kent, let's face it, were oot fir whit they could get, if ahm bein honest. That's whit smart folk are aw aboot. It's a sign o the times, if ye ask me. Or mebbe it's always been like that.

So, when Minty startit hearin the voice, she took it as a sign. The voice belonged tae a singer called Benedict Kerna. Good name eh? He sang wi a group called Glory Hand an they played knicker shittin, crashin guitar, screamin lyric rock... but wi a tune, y'know?

I was intae heavy dance beats maself, an takin a few E's - so I didnae bother much wi Glory Hand. But I mind one time Minty makin me listen tae some o Kerna's lyrics.

So I run and I hide, when I find no solace inside
And I sold myself on the soft soul sell
Now I'm sitting here waiting for the finishing bell
And I crave and I breed,
I stalk my prey and I feed
And I'm making love like there's no tomorrow
And guess what? There's no tomorrow.

Shite eh? But he had a no bad voice... like sugar burning in a jar. I cannae really describe it.

I remember the day I first kent somethin was awfy wrong an awfy right wi ma sister, if that makes ony sense. She wis goin wi this lad called Jimmy Chapman an they must hae had a barny or somethin - I think they finished or maybe he hit hir. I dinnae ken. I was doon the pub an come back an heard this thumpin, soon as I got in the door - like the hoose hid a heart. I snuck up the stair an went intae Minty's bedroom. She wis standin at the window, wi the light on. Good job we only overlooked a bunch of coos, cause she jist had on a wee t-shirt an a pair of knickers. That wis aboot it.

Ye ken the scene fae *Poltergeist* where aw the stuff flies aboot the room? It was like that, except it wis the racket bouncin aff the walls an no the furniture. Glory Hand wis playin so loud it pushed mah eyelashes back against mah heid. Minty had hold o the windowsill an she wis... screamin. Aye, screamin at the tap o' her lungs an hoppin up an doon like an epileptic elf, shakin her head fae side to side, so tears whipped across the windowpanes an left miserable streaks on the glass.

She seen ma reflection an jerked roond an, I'm tellin ye, I wis aboot tae run. But she was smilin. Smilin an howlin an greetin at the same time - an through aw that, she managed tae gie me some kind o signal, I think.

Dinnae ask whit. A wee glimpse o her real self maybe? It wis half-welcoming, half defiant. Half-human? All human? I dinnae ken whit it was. But I smiled back an... a stupid thing... I gave her a sort o Saturday night TV talk show thumbs up, as I backed oot the door. So she blew me a kiss.

She was aw right, mah sister.

That got me wonderin. I thought I was awfy good wi girls cause I could get the pants off them, but maybe that was wrong. I wasnae bothered aboot feelings, except for feelin boobs. But I didnae have tae act the shit, even if I couldnae give one. It's no right tae piss yer girl aboot, just cause ye think you can make it up later.

I still did it, like. But less. Tried a wee bit harder.

After all, whit a guy ye would be if ye never let anyone doon! Eh? People wid point at ye in the street. Like I said, it's a wee toon.

Anyway, that's how Minty fell in love wi Benedict Kerna. The man spoke poetry tae her an he wasnae around, so he would never let her doon. Good, eh?

So what did the poor bastard do? He let her doon.

He killed hisself.

But the bastard couldnae just fuck off and die, could he? Naw, he hid tae be the big fuckin man aboot it... Hurtin ma wee sister an managin tae make it look like he wis doin her a favour. Openin her eyes, an the like.

Men... eh?

He left a suicide note. Left it for Minty an aw his ither stupit wee groupies what worshipped him. The newspapers published it.

I can't live any more in a shitty world like this. If I thought my life and my music would change things, I would stay. But I reckon my death will achieve more. My parents and yours live in the big house on the hill with the picket (barbed wire) fence. Like the rest of their generation, they've given up changing things. I hope my death will help them live again. Follow me, if you have the vision. Our parents are as lost as our children will be - if we do not show them we are willing to sacrifice ourselves for our brother, our sister, our world. Let us show our elders what they have done to their children. Peace to you all. And courage.

He wrote it on Instagram. Sign o the times, eh?

Suddenly the guy was the fuckin spokesman for a lost generation. They even had a couple of discussions aboot it on Saturday night TV. Minty an ma faither watched. Big Don wis spoutin his philosophy on the hale shebang, drappin bitties o Custard Cream doon his beard an makin 'stiff' jokes. Minty wis sayin nothin. I wisnae bothered.

Then a mental thing happened. Some girl topped hirsel. Jill Ingles wis her name, I think. Then another one. Dead as a tattie scone.

Bang. Media ootcry. Then mair suicides wi angry notes. Change the world. Kill yourself. Make your faithers listen.

Good, eh?

The papers got fine an outraged. Whit a circus. There wis a bigger headline every day.

Tragedy of Sad Fan, Fiona – 16

Watery, hypocritical pish like that jist pissed off aw the other sad Fionas' mair.

Within a month, there were seven girls dead. It was crazy. It was a fuckin epidemic. Faithers on Saturday night TV givin it the big sniffles an moaning *whit had they done*? And how they didnae understand.

I tend tae think that was the whole point. One auld lad got interviewed. I'll aye mind his name, an I'm no very good with names. John Jambuscha. He didnae hae much tae say, jist that he thought his dead daughter was right. If he didnae change his life an dae his bit tae help the world, her death would've been in vain.

The next day another three lassies were gone and the papers were laying intae John Jambuscha like he'd advocated fistin the Pope. He got sued by one of the irate faithers. I dinnae ken whit happened tae him after that.

A girl called Gwen Cooper cut her wrists. Left a letter sayin she'd written twenty times tae the Fisheries Commission, protesting aboot whaling fleets trawlin the North Sea, or somethin. She never got a reply. Poor cunt just got fed up waiting.

Her father turned up at the hoose of the head of the Fisheries Commission an stabbed him in the chest.

The authorities went ape. Glory Hand's records were banned. That helped a lot, right? Panic in the streets, babies gettin eaten. Oh aye, a bonafide national emergency. At the next regional elections, the government lost the greatest number of seats in party history.

Good, eh? I went doon the pub tae celebrate an got pished.

When I came home, ma faither wis still oot drinking. The hoose wis thumping again. Upstairs Minty's door was open.

She wis hanging fae the light. Her nose had bin bleedin an I told reporters that the circling of her body dripped a wee heart of blood on the floor underneath. It wasnae true. I jist wanted folk tae remember her.

Big Don's grief was mighty tae behold, so I got oot afore he started carving everybody slices of blame, an hagglin over who would get the biggest share.

I hired a wee flat. It wis time tae be a writer now that somethin had actually happened tae me. But I never got roond tae finishing anything and ended up a salesman.

Now my faither hid nae wife, nae daughter an nae me. At last, he had unlimited pub time and a TV all to himself. But, d'ye think that bastard took it on the chin? Like hell he did.

Naw. He wrote a song aboot Minty. Called it *Chocolate* of course. Wanker.

He couldnae even play an instrument, so he sent his dippy sang tae one of those 'fix-it' programmes on Saturday night TV - and they thought it would be a grand idea if aw the faithers o the dead girls sang it together. Good eh?

When they went on TV I got drunk again. It was the only way I could get tae grips with it.

I wish she'd walk right through the door
Walk right down our street once more
Pointing out the sights as if I hear her
She'd tell me how she spent her day
The things she did or didn't say
As if she hadn't gone away
As if I'm near her.

As bad as bloody Glory Hand. Some Japanese record company offered tae release it. The profits would go intae a charitable fund dedicated to the Dead Daughters of the Revolution. That's the nickname I gave them. The newspapers called those poor wee corpsettes the 'Rock Follies' for a while, then stopped when they got blamed fur encouraging mair deaths.

Big Don's band called themselves The Cross and wore wee blue crosses as a sign of mourning. After performing on a couple of Saturday night chat shows they had a bunch of big rock stars ready to sing on the single with them.

'Chocolate' went tae number one.

Fat women in summer floral dresses and a million everyday Jock Thomsons, who never even knew her, put flowers on Minty's grave.

What a sad fuckin testament tae a beautiful lassie.

I expected The Cross tae fade away. They didnae. They made another single. And you know what? It was good. Ma faither was a no bad singer. Had a voice like sugar burning in a jar.

After the second hit there weren't any more suicides.

Sometimes I like tae say my father had somethin to do with that. Sometimes I say I hope to God he didnae. Depends on how sozzled I am.

That's how dad makes his living these days. He dumped The Cross when their popularity started to fade, learned guitar and now he's a staple on tacky Saturday night TV variety shows. He's rich and in his seventies. Got a kindly old folk crooner countenance aboot him, all cardies and white ruggy hair. Does the odd duet with Bono just to keep his hand in.

I quit sales. It was an even more scurrying, ratlike thing than the real world. I ended up managing a wee handcraft shop in a village up north. I'll not even bother to name it. You wouldn't find it on a map.

I got married. Bonny girl. Sincere. The kind that likes a bit of distance between herself and the harsh realities of life.

We don't want children. She paints landscapes just for me an helps in the shop, and I still write a bit – though I wouldn't let anyone but her read it. Big Don visits now and then but gets fed up when he cannae get a sing-song going.

So... my wife and I, we live here. The years go by, and we watch them pass, like spots of blood dripping into a heart - I can't really describe it. We don't have a

TV. I think we're hoping we can get through our lives before civilization rolls over us.

Two whales, that's her an me. We've got no place to go and nothin to do. We just hang about here, waiting and circling, singing undeciphered songs to each other, in our ever shrinking ocean.

People think I'm not bothered.

Good, eh?

Christmas Day In the Morning

Last thing anyone wants to do is work Christmas Day, me especially. Then again... defence of the realm and everything.

Aye. There I was defending the realm on Christmas Eve, in the shape of Edinburgh Castle, and it looked like I was going to be defending it on Christmas Day an all. I was feeling sorry for myself, stuck out here in the cold, in front of this big stupid portcullis. Whoever it was invented the wind tunnel was standing in front of Edinburgh Castle when he got the idea, I bet. All I had for shelter was my wee guard box and I wasn't even allowed to stand inside it.

I shifted the M55 away from my cheek before it stuck to the metal. Not as impressive a weapon as the iron cannons bristling on the ramparts above, but just as bloody cold. I scanned the empty car park for signs of invasion and tried to think about military tactics. If you attack a castle on Christmas Eve, do you bring your presents, in case you win? And, if this place is such a great defensive fortress, how come I have to guard it from the outside?

Ach, our squad were just here this time of year to give tourists something to photograph, that and stopping punters nicking the valuables. And who's going to try sneaking the crown jewels out under their coat on Christmas Eve from a castle filled with soldiers wearing mini-kilts, freezing their own crown jewels and so narked off they'd probably welcome an attack just so's they could work off their aggression and get a bit warm?

Shows how wrong you can be.

The clock at St. Giles' struck five. The last die-hard tourists would have to leave soon and I could hear Big Tam, Chalky, Wee Davie and Gack muttering their way from the stone guardhouse, stamping out fags on the slippery cobbles, and heading into the darkening interior of Edinburgh Castle to round up stragglers. Not that there were many visitors. As far as I could remember, the only folk that had passed through the gates were the obligatory trio of Japanese, a long-haired kid with a skateboard and some shivering American woman, starling thin, getting dragged round by an overenthusiastic husband.

"Look, honey, this building is older than our entire country!"

Big deal. I've got biscuits in the staff cupboard older than their entire country.

Oh, and there was a bunch of Italian teenagers on some organised tour, less interested in being here than me, if that were heavenly possible. I hate Italian kids. They'll lie on the ground and take pictures right up your kilt. Spanish kids do it, too. And the French. So much for the Auld Alliance.

Dumb anyway, us having to wear undies. All right, I appreciate them keeping my tackle warm but it seems a shame, a Scottish soldier's greatest weapon not being always at hand to scare the enemy. I bet that's why soldiers were called privates in the first place.

An alarm rang inside the castle, breaking into my musings. An alarm? No. Surely, it must be the closing bell. Only we don't *have* a closing bell. They might have got one in and not bothered to tell me. That wouldn't be unusual around here.

I unshouldered my gun and walked cautiously back through the giant entrance, the light from the open guardhouse door illuminating a million tiny parachutes of snow, as they drifted to their deaths in the glistening courtyard. A wide cobbled road - laid by French prisoners during the Napoleonic Wars, so I'd heard - wound steeply up through layers of secondary walls into the castle's inner defences.

Grasping my rifle tighter, I trotted up the hill, lifting my knees as high as I could. These tackety boots are pretty slidy and I had a bayonet on the end of my gun. I mean, it's filed down so's not to take out some tourist's eye, but there's no sense in being reckless. I slid my heels sideways with each downward footfall to gain extra traction. That's how highland dancing started, I bet.

Then, about three-quarters of the way up the slope, the strangest sight materialised out of the darkness. The kid with the skateboard, the one I'd noticed earlier, was whizzing down the winding cobbled walkway on his favoured mode of transport. I didn't recognise him at first, cause his long blonde hair was tucked into the Crown of Scotland. It bobbed violently up and down on his head, as he tried to hold it in place with one hand. In the other, he grasped the jewelled Sceptre of the Kingdom, thrust out like a lance.

Quite a sense of balance, that kid.

Big Tam, Chalky and Gack popped up on a wall, high above the steep grass verge that bordered the walkway. They unslung their guns and aimed at the fleeing jewel thief.

"Hey, youz... Stop!" Chalky shouted down. "Stop, or we'll have tae kill ye!"

"Aye, ya wee bam." Big Tam added threateningly. "Dinnae be a tool!"

Wee Davie appeared on the north wall, on the other side of the cobbled road, waving his arms at the rifles opposite.

"What if he doesnae speak English, ya eedjits?" he yelled, jumping up and down, with his kilt birling around him.

"Whit? You mean he couldnae read that muckle sign sayin *Dinnae Steal the Crown Jewels*?" Chalky was unrepentant.

"Och, no man, but mebbie he doesnae realise the seriousness of his situation!"

The wee skateboarder hurtled past me on the left only to find himself heading for the hulking form of Sgt. Major Wilson, legs apart and handlebar moustache laden with frost, filling the archway at the bottom of the walk, like some turn of the century goalie. He thrust out his bayonet and grinned maniacally.

"I'd say the wee bawbag is aware of his situation noo," Chalky cackled.

As acknowledgement that he did indeed grasp the precariousness of his position, the skateboarder executed a perfect 90-degree turn and shot up the grass embankment. Sgt. Major Wilson moved out from the gate, tattooed arms wide, to catch the intruder once gravity pulled him back. The skateboarder promptly did another spectacular turn and shot down behind Sgt. Major Wilson, giving him a hefty dunt on the head with the sceptre. He sprawled across the slippery stone, kilt up round his neck, and a quickly stifled cheer rose from the riflemen on the ramparts.

"I seen Pele make that exact same move in the 1977 world cup," Big Tam remarked, not without some reverence.

The skateboarder sailed through the archway and the riflemen rushed along the parapet so's not to lose sight of him. I ran past Sgt. Major Wilson's prone figure, in time to see the young thief continuing his suicidal journey downhill.

"Shoot at his bloody wheels!" Wee Davie's voice drifted down to the left of me.

"Shoot the wheels?" Chalky yelled back from the right. "He's on a skateboard! What do you think I am, a sodding marksman?"

"Shoot the whole fucking skateboard then!"

"He's bouncing up and down like a Leith prossie! I cannae get a line on it."

"You're lucky this isn't the 1970s, man." Big Tam's voice joined in above. "In the 70s, skateboards were a lot smaller. I fell off one and fractured my skull. Mind you," he added sagely. "I wasnae even wearing a helmet, never mind a big, padded crown."

"Shoot any bit of him you like!" screamed Sgt. Major Wilson, struggling to his feet. "Just stop the wee nyaff!"

"He's heading for those Italian lassies!" Chalky roared. "Hey, youz! Senoritas! Hasta dal vista... partez le boditas! Aw crap! Go on youz, will ye? Vitte... vitte!"

The Italians got the message, more from the pointing guns than the eloquence of Chalky's warning. They ran back and forwards, banging into each other and trying to surrender.

Though he'd had few problems eluding our entire squad, the skateboarder was no match for a bunch of screaming Italian teenagers, running full tilt into a particularly portly lass and coming to an immediate standstill. Having lost the momentum to carry him past the main gate, he flipped the skateboard into one arm with a well-practised flick of his foot and ran towards a set of ancient stone steps that wound back up into the heart of the castle.

"That was a nice wee move, an all," said Big Tam. "Boy's a born footballer."

Behind us, the alarm was still ringing.

Big Tam, Chalky and Gack came sliding down the grass verge out of the darkness, grimacing and gasping every time their buttocks touched the freezing grass. By the time we got to the main entrance, the fugitive was halfway up the steps, skateboard under one arm and sceptre still in his hand.

Sgt. Major Wilson caught up with us, three more squaddies in tow. They swung their rifles at the blonde criminal, now vanishing into the night at the top of the stairs.

"Fire!" screamed Sgt. Major Wilson.

There was a flurry of clicks.

"We're no allowed live ammo while tourists are still in the castle," Wee Davie reminded him.

"Right!" screamed Sgt. Major Wilson, his dreams of promotion sliding faster than the herd of bleating Italians up the cobbles towards us. "McDuff, Banks, MacDonald, get those bloody Eyeties out the front gate and lock it. Hardy... break out the real ammo, take the rest of the squad and start combing the grounds. You three... up the stairs an after that hairy bugger. Shoot to kill. Dinnae hit the crown, mind."

Me, Big Tam, Gack and Chalky thundered up the narrow stone steps after our prey, heading towards the forbidding black spires of the castle's inner fortifications. We loaded the hastily gathered ammo as we went, kilts swinging and hearts pounding. This was rare, the first time I had felt good and toasty all day. Chalky and I grinned at each other and took the last stairs three at a time.

Then we were through the dank portal of the inner wall and into the highest and most ancient courtyard. To the left, standing meekly on its own and dwarfed by the thick walls of war, stood St. Margaret's Chapel, the oldest building in Edinburgh. Directly in front of us was the sheer frontage of the war memorial rooms, tall deep shadows studded with angular soulless windows. On the right, as solid and unimposing as the artefact it sheltered, squatted a converted stable that housed the Stone of Scone – though it was only there for cleaning. Usually it was locked safely away in the same room as the crown jewels, which the wee lad had just managed to steal. So, a fat lot of good that would have done, anyway.

We didn't want to split up, seeing how handy the skateboarder was with that sceptre and us not having the chance to use live ammunition much. Instead, we were about to light a couple of Marlboros and shout down for reinforcements when we heard a feeble cheer coming from the left. When we looked closer, we could see a faint ethereal light shining out of one of the cross latticed stable windows. Nodding to each other, we shoved the cigarettes behind our ears and, pointing our rifles, burst through the door. My glasses fogged up straight away and I got tangled in what felt like some kind of information rack.

"Would you get the bayonet oot my face?" Big Tam swatted me away. "I can see that's a nice postcard of a heelan coo stuck on the end of it."

Chalky turned me round so I was facing in the right direction.

Then the mist on my specs cleared and I was looking at a stranger sight than any I had seen that night, which was certainly saying something.

The young skateboarder was sitting cross-legged on top of the Stone of Scone, the Scottish crown now set straight on top of his head. In one hand he held the sceptre. In the other, a cigarette, grey wispy smoke curling into the air and matching the colour of the mucky stone under him. The skateboarder's sneakered feet protruded from wide plaid pants and, at those feet, hands clasped, knelt the all-American husband I'd seen earlier. His wife, standing to one side, looked as resigned as she had been when struggling along the windswept battlements, in search of our cleverly hidden information plaques. But her hubby seemed rather enraptured by the whole tableau. In the background were the three Japanese tourists, cameras at the ready in case anything happened, or even if it didn't.

"Right, wee man. Get doon aff that stane." Big Tam pointed his weapon at the skateboarder.

"Excuse me officer, Sir." The American raised a finger. "I don't think you can legally arrest my client."

"Of course not." Tam looked puzzled. "We're the army. All we can do is shoot him."

He motioned with his gun. "C'mon. hop to it."

"Client?" I asked. "What do you mean, client?"

The American had a business card out of his wallet and in front of my nose before my trigger finger could twitch.

"Frank Beezlebum. From the offices of Beezlebum, Fayed and Chang. Attorneys at law."

"Bloody ambeerlance chaser." Gack frowned. "And how long has this wee toerag been your client?"

"About two minutes. See, look at this." He unfolded a crumpled paper. "The young gentleman gave it to me just now. It's his family tree."

"Red crayon. That's nice."

"No, look here, I mean." He held up the scrap. "I've become a bit of an expert on genealogy."

"Dirty bugger," Gack grunted.

"That's gynaecology, Gack."

"Yeah. I been over here tracing my Scottish ancestry. Turns out my great, great grandfather was a midden keeper in Banff, whatever that means."

Frank's wife sighed. Frank waved the paper at us.

"If this is right, and it looks to be, this young man is the direct descendent of the Count of Roehenstart who was *supposed* to have died without an heir in a riding accident in 1854. This fellow claims he didn't."

"And?"

"The Count of Roehenstart was the son of Augustus Edward Maximilian de Roehenstart and the Duchess of Albany."

"So?"

Frank Beezlebum heaved a sigh, despairing at this ignorance of our own history.

"Augustus Edward Maximilian de Roehenstart was the great-grandson of Charles II of Britain. The Duchess of Albany was Charlotte Stuart, daughter of Bonnie Prince Charlie. That gives him Royal Stuart blood on both sides."

Frank took his glasses off and wiped them furiously.

"If what he says is true, this kid has a perfectly legitimate claim to the throne of your country. And he's just crowned himself in front of a bunch of witnesses."

Frank's wife sighed again. The Japanese tourists bowed and took some more photographs.

"It's a legal minefield, I'll admit, but I wouldn't shoot this young man if I was you... or even try to touch him. It could be construed as an act of treason."

The lawyer smiled his best courtroom smile.

"It's quite possible that he's the true king of Scotland."

Oscar Stewart smiled, too, and took a drag on his cigarette.

Christmas Eve.

I'm standing on the ramparts of Edinburgh Castle, rifle in hand, staring out into the gloom. Sgt. Major Wilson has given us all 300 rounds of live ammunition and allowed the few English members of our squad safe passage out of the gates, including Big Tam, who suddenly claimed to have been born in Tunbridge Wells.

Chalky and Wee Davie have taken down the Union Jack and put up the Lion Rampart and Scottish flag instead. Sgt. Major Wilson informed his superiors by field radio that, as a Scots regiment, we were bound by duty to protect our king and country. And, since that country maybe had a new king, we would be occupying the military garrison of Edinburgh Castle until the situation could be appraised, whatever that meant.

I doubt anyone will try and storm the walls right away. It's Christmas and the castle's too nice to damage. But we've broken out the gas masks in case of a sneaky attack.

In the courtyard below me, the soldiers are gathered round a fire, playing cards with the new boy king. The Japanese are taking instant Polaroids and handing them out as presents. Mrs Lawyer is heating up a bowl of soup for Oscar Stewart and her husband is discussing a possible invasion of England with Sgt. Major Wilson.

Although it's a legal minefield, he claims the house of Stewart still has a legitimate claim on the throne of Britain.

Over my shoulder, the soft halo of dawn begins to rise. The stars and the lights of the city finally separate and define themselves. Smoke rises from the chimneys and Princes Street glistens like a grimy jewelled crown.

Looks like I *will* be guarding Edinburgh Castle on Christmas Day.

The Last Thylacine

Granddad was small and brown, like a crumpled paper bag, and lived in a home. Dad made me visit once a month, though he didn't come himself. He said they didn't get on.

When dad was my age, granddad took him and gran to Australia to seek their fortune. He was going to have his own fish van, like at home, because a lot of Australia was inland and he thought they'd appreciate a balanced diet. But he overslept on the boat and they ended up in Tasmania.

There weren't many people there and fish tended to go off quickly in the heat, so he never got rich. He could only afford a tiny wooden shack near the beach. It got too much for granny and eventually, they all came back to Aberdeen. But my dad still hates the seaside and can't pass a garden shed without wincing.

When I arrived at the home, granddad was sitting in a tatty robe, looking at old photographs. Some were of gran before she passed away. I picked one up. Gran was standing on the edge of a steamy Tasmanian forest, looking young. Beside her frolicked granddad's dog, a big collie called Mumphy.

Beside Grandma was the strangest animal I'd ever seen. It looked like a dog, too, but had huge gaping jaws and tiger stripes up its back.

"That," granddad said solemnly. "Is a Thylacine."

Granddad rarely smiled.

"What's a Thylacine?"

"Look it up on that internet thing."

Then he went back to his pictures. Granddad was never one for talking.

So I did. According to the website, Thylacines were also called Tasmanian Wolves had stripy back legs and huge, powerful jaws. The last ever Thylacine died in Hobart Zoo in 1936.

I knew granddad was old, but he wasn't *that* old. I ran back to the home.

"You and Grandma found a living Thylacine in Tasmania!" I said. "You could have been rich after all. You could have been famous!"

"We didn't tell anyone," he replied. "The authorities would just have dragged the poor creature off to another zoo." He picked up the photograph and sighed. I couldn't tell if he was looking at the last Thylacine or gran.

"All he wanted was what I wanted," granddad said. "A bit of freedom. A space to roam."

He put the photograph back in his old shoebox and shut the lid.

I went outside. My own dog, Mumphy III, was tied to a tree. He was a collie cross, and his mother and his mother's mother had all belonged to my family.

Mumphy III had tufty fur and pricked-up ears, like all collies, but there were darker bands on his back and legs. I always thought they looked a bit weird. He gave a loud yawn and I noticed for the first time that his jaw was awfully large.

I glanced up at the windows of the home. Granddad was watching from behind the glass.

He smiled, just once, and gave a little bow.

After that, I kind of liked my granddad.

Bang Snap

Santana and Wodoom were playing Bang Snap. Wodoom hung over a vast starry array, brow furrowed in concentration.

"C'mon," Santana urged. "You haven't made a move in millennia. No wonder this game is taking so long."

He held up a sketch pad.

"Hey, look. I've created a race called the Queewhiggly. They're basically ears with wings. And they're deaf!"

"Oh, thou art hilarious." Wodoom wiggled his pinkie, sending an asteroid crashing into a tiny blue sphere. "Bet thou didst not see *that* coming, though."

"Oi! That was one of my favourite planets." Santana threw up his hands. "It had Netflix."

The Bus Pass of Dorian Gray

"You must be joking, pal," the driver sniffed. "This hideous old geezer don't look nuffink like you."

He scratched under the arm of his white polyester shirt.

"Off you get, before I put me foot up yer arse."

Dorian sighed and started walking instead.

A Monster Circles the Wreckage

*Serial killers are not radicals: they have enthusias-
tically embraced the established order only to discover
that it offers them no place they can endure. Encalcu-
lated with an ambition which they are either unable to
attain or cannot feel at ease living.*

Dr. Elliot Leyton. *Hunting Humans.*

*I didn't think or realise I would ever do these
things... I never really wanted to hurt anybody... what
drove me to do this? I don't think I was born like this.
Why did I start?*

Albert De Salvo, The Boston Strangler.

"You know. There are two types of criminals."
Miles Harrison was seated in the captain's chair,
though the oxygen tank strapped to his back meant he
had to perch on the edge. "Some think their biggest
mistake was getting caught. Others believe it was getting born."

He glanced at Stuart.

"Aren't you going to take notes?"

"Oh, very droll." Stuart's arm was missing just above the elbow. "Don't worry. I won't forget this shit-show in a hurry."

A slow spiral of blood floated up from the ragged stump, diluted by water. From behind his mask, Miles could see the cabin had taken on a rose-tinted hue.

"Due to the circumstances, I'm going to be fairly direct," Stuart said. "I don't wanna... just circle the subject."

"Not like our friend outside, huh?"

As if on cue, a huge dark mass drifted past the window, momentarily blocking the weak light. Miles was almost out of air but he had no intention of venturing beyond the cabin while that creature lurked in the gloom. Stuart followed it with his eyes.

"Looks like this is your last chance to come clean."

"You want to know why I killed these women?" Miles thought for a while. "I think it was cause of a novel I was trying to write. Or maybe there wasn't much on TV these nights. In the end, all roads lead to Rome, Stuart."

He checked the cylinder gauge. Well below the caution zone. And he had so much to say. The two men obviously couldn't hear each other, yet communication didn't seem to be a problem. Maybe because of encroaching Hypoxia. Maybe because Stuart had died half an hour ago.

"Nazis!" Miles decided a tirade would be fastest. "Let me tell you about Nazis, Stu. Wore nice uniforms.

Invaded Poland. What about those former blue-eyed boys?"

He put on a cut-glass English accent.

"How could the rotten Jerry persecute those poor homeless Jews? Bad form. Filthy Hun. Only Jews aren't poor or homeless anymore, says Facebook. No. Now they're controlling America or persecuting poor homeless Palestinians."

"That's Israelis. There's a distinction."

"Don't muddy the waters." Miles laughed mirthlessly. "Every man on the street knows, if we all gave an itsy bitsy, teeny weeny yellow polka dot bit of our wages to the Third World, we could wipe out famine. Cheese off our little suburban dicks. Do we do it?"

"I guess not," his companion admitted.

"Course not! We've endless excuses. I don't wanna be encouraging these people to have more kids - not with a global famine on! They overpopulate their world and, next thing you know, they're over here overpopulating ours. Turn back the fuckers' boats! Let 'em drown!"

He gave the instrument console a muffled thump.

"How do you think this nasty old tub ended up down here? It was already a grave before I discovered the wreck. I just added to it."

"How efficient of you. Also, a bit simplistic in the analogy department."

"Aw, don't tell me you people can't see the big picture. You're all sitting high enough up on white, middle-class picket fences."

"I wasn't going to," Stuart began. But Miles was on a roll.

"There's always a war going on somewhere, so you might have to become a Nazi, or you'll end up skulking in the ghetto. But you gotta be careful, eh? When a soldier fires at the enemy, he's a patriot. By the time the bullet has reached its victim, yet another ceasefire has been declared and he's a murderer. Ends up on death row, waiting for the state to execute *him*."

The oxygen gauge gave a bleep. Miles forced himself to calm down.

"We're allowed to kill, Stuart. I just didn't get the proper permission."

"Right. Thanks." Stuart's face remained impassive, but a slight eddy caught his wispy hair and wafted it upwards. It gave the impression he was horrified and trying not to show it. "I should have had you over for a Xmas lunch. Not just a provocative raconteur but an expert on carving. We could have eaten spleen with a nice bottle of Chianti."

"Call it the times, or genetics or our upbringing but we're as much a mass product as the processed meat on any supermarket counter." Miles ignored the sarcasm. "Future generations will probably look back on us eating animals with the same disgust we have for people who kept slaves."

"So... You were writing down your fantasies." Stuart refused to be side-tracked. "Then you acted them out. Would that be right?"

"No. Not at all."

"What then? Your pencil snapped and you did too?"

"Once things are down on paper, they come a little closer to being real, yes. But what I wrote didn't make me want to kill anyone. Course not. It just set my mind on a certain track. See, I stopped asking myself *what makes people kill* and started asking *what stops them from doing it*? Y'know? I seriously thought about it."

"And what stops them from doing it?"

"Circumstances mainly. And another reason."

"What's that?"

"They never seriously thought about doing it."

Outside the window, the leviathan made another pass, looking for some way to reach them. But the aluminium and fibreglass of the fishing boat's cabin had held up well, despite years under the sea, though the wooden panels were rotted and covered in barnacles. The compass was overgrown with moss and the steering wheel had fallen off long ago. It lay on the floor like a spiky, tarnished halo.

"Awright." Stuart flourished an imaginary pen. "An awkward question. For an... ah... obviously intelligent guy. Well... your jobs..."

"Shit, huh?"

"Not exactly rocket science."

"I got bored easily. What's the difference between cleaning a toilet and curing cancer? One takes a lot longer. You never felt like that?"

"I suppose."

"Well, I'm more unsettled than you and you had a better job than me."

"I didn't, really." The man looked abashed. "I didn't make a lot of money."

"Shame. You would have, after this."

"What would you *like* to have done?"

"Avoided killing people, mainly."

"Ehm... apart from that?"

"I dunno. Something creative. Not writing, though. I gave that up. It's too cerebral. Too many notes, Mozart. That's why I asked you to tell my story."

"But you pinned your hopes on writing at one time?"

"I figured if I could get things published, that would set me up in a lot of ways. I could earn money and still not be stuck, y'know?"

"But you never got anything published."

"Nothing," Miles chuckled. "Not even my novel about a Goddamned serial killer. Guess it didn't ring true."

His head had begun to ache, so he checked the gauge again. It was firmly in the red. His arms felt sluggish, though he was hardly in the same boat as Stuart. Then again, he was.

Miles began to giggle.

"Around the time you went... off the rails," Stuart said tactfully. "You were seeing a woman. Ally Stone. 28 years old."

He glanced at imaginary notes.

"Pretty young."

"Thank you. There were a couple of others, but they were casual."

"You shittin me?"

"I'd got that 'deep but fun' thing down pat. The 'hint of badness' that girls love."

"Yeah. If you're still living in the 1990s."

"Perhaps I was. Upshot of my environment and all that. Guess those girls didn't take the hint."

"I'm surprised you could get it up so often." Stuart's eyebrow arched and a couple of small bubbles drifted off, as if he'd had a cartoonish thought. "You could... couldn't you?"

Miles raised his own eyebrows in return.

"Forget it." Stuart grimaced. "I don't need to know every tiny little detail."

"Specially not if you're gonna phrase it like that. And don't be naive. My motivations were... complex."

"Was your sexual relationship with Ally a good one, then?"

"I'd say so."

"But... something must have been missing."

"You still think the adoring public has to know the size of my member?" Miles pursed his lips.

"No. You keep that under your hat, metaphorically speaking." Stuart gave an annoyed snort. "Besides, nobody's gonna read about you now."

Miles let the barb pass.

"I don't know. I guess sex was never a be-all and end-all for me. I mean, there's a brief period after the initial nervousness and the eventual... boredom when screwing someone is great." He hesitated. "All right, boredom's too strong a word. Having nothing new to show them and them to show you."

He raised a hand to his brow as if scanning unknown horizons.

"The first few times, you're both explorers. After that..."

"New lands to explore?"

"That's right. But I was getting old, Stuart. Way past my prime. A salty old dog with nothing but stories of previous encounters, slowly turning into a ruin of his former self."

"With a lover 20 years your junior." His companion sounded envious. "Doesn't sound so bad."

"She'd find a younger me, eventually. Too many wrinkles, Mozart." Miles patted his face. "Don't underestimate the call of the sea. Plenty more fish there."

"And what do explorers do when the only new lands left are hostile?"

"They attack and subdue them."

"Much as I appreciate these nautical metaphors, you gonna kiss and tell?"

"Nothing to say. I loved Ally and she loved me. She even asked me to go to America with her. But the age gap was huge and she wasn't the settling-down type either. Then what? I... I... had a job here."

"That's right. You were head of Microsoft."

"In the end, she wouldn't want some old guy hanging on her coat tails." Miles flicked his flippers and rose a few inches, hovering over the seat. "You know what happens when you try to be Peter Pan? People stop believing in you and you fade away."

He sank back down and looked around. There were five female corpses in the corner of the cabin, weighed down by chains around their necks. Prey to every passing marine animal, none of them had faces. Miles tried hard to think but most of their names eluded him. Due to lack of air, he presumed. Or perhaps he had never known. His lungs were starting to hurt.

"Tell me about the women, Miles." Stuart broke into his reverie. "It's time."

"Let's see. If you took all the girls I slept with and laid them end to end, about a dozen would get run over on the highway."

"Being flippant isn't helping your case."

"I didn't mean to kill the first one, you know." Miles shrugged. "I was just getting my own back and it spiralled out of control."

"Getting your own back. You wanted revenge on society."

"I wanted revenge on *her*." Miles searched his memory. "I was at an ATM with Ally. She was being too slow or too flamboyant, I don't know."

"How can you be flamboyant at an ATM?"

"Ally could, trust me. Anyway, there were a couple of young girls behind us. Tall, blonde, out for the night. Cleavage like the Bermuda triangle. Started slagging Ally. Maybe it was the way she was dressed. Or just trying to cause trouble. I told one of them to shut it and, bang, the boyfriend was there - acting like he should've been on top of the Empire State Building swatting planes. Right up in my face, he was."

Miles leaned forwards and rasped out a Brooklyn accent.

You looking at me, huh? You fuckin looking at me?

"You were attacked by Robert De Niro?"

"He's the only tough guy I can imitate."

"Did you get into a fight?"

"Nah. I hate violence. Anyhow, a couple of months later, I saw one of those girls again, going into her apartment. Then I knew where she lived. I kept watch on her house a couple of times, sort of like a game."

"A game?" Stuart frowned.

"I kinda thought I could use it as research for my book. To follow someone and secretly watch them. I wanted that novel so much to be a success. Thought I had a unique perspective."

"I'd certainly go along with that."

"I needed to really experience what a fledgling killer would. You're writing about me, after all. Don't you want to be accurate? But you won't understand how I feel, no matter how much I describe it. You'd have to...

"Let's stick with the narrative," Stuart interrupted. "I'll live."

He glanced at his missing arm.

"That was a dumb thing to say."

"All right, maybe I was thinking of some way I could get back at her." Miles' face crumpled. "I only wanted to frighten her. Take some money. I was broke. She hurt other people without a second thought. Why shouldn't she have the tables turned? She gave up her right to safety, picking on Ally like that. I don't know. I had a million reasons."

"Too many notes, Mozart?"

"Yeah. Anyway, she came home late one night. Short skirt. Staggering a bit. I'd been drinking. She'd been drinking."

He clenched his fists and pounded his head.

"To this day, I still don't know where I found the nerve. I wish to God I hadn't. But I crawled through the window. Slammed into her coming out of the bedroom and there was no turning back."

He closed his eyes.

"I tied her to a kitchen chair and gagged her. I had a mask on and went looking for cash. She was making whimpering noises in the next room, reminding me she was there. I only wanted to let her see what it's like to be threatened. I leaned over her, pretending like I was going to do something to scare her. Moved my hands down over her breasts. To show her what it's like being abused by a stranger."

He looked at the floor.

"And... maybe cause I wanted to feel them."

"Miles..."

"I just... kept going." He raised his head defiantly. "You play dog eat dog, a bigger animal might just come along and gobble you up. Too many dogs, Mozart."

"Don't start telling me you ate your victims." Stuart looked distinctly queasy. "I'll probably barf."

"Not at all. I always knew I wasn't quite right, though." Miles seemed properly reflective for a second. "I mean, I could act like the nicest guy in the world but my best friend might be pouring her heart out to me, and if there was a song I liked on the radio..."

"Half your brain would be listening to that."

"All of it. Then again, I'm a big music fan."

"And a complete sociopath."

"Well, duh! That's why you have to cover up your flaws." Miles gave a charming smile, though it was hidden by his mouthpiece. "Nobody likes flaws. Everyone pretends, to some extent. No honey! You're not too fat... ya big sweaty beast. Of course, I wouldn't fuck your sister... unless she let me. We all think horrible thoughts and pretend we don't, so why not go for broke? Why not do exactly what we want to do and pretend we don't? Not hurting someone's feelings is much more important than truth."

"I'd say killing these women went a damn sight further than hurting their feelings." Stuart was stone-faced. "Don't *you* have feelings to hurt?"

"I know how to feel lots of things," Miles retorted. "I know how to feel like an outsider. I know how to feel like a failure. I know how to feel incomplete. I know how to feel scared. I know how to feel useless. I know how to feel cheated. I know how to feel lonely."

He grunted sourly.

"And I know how to pretend that I don't."

"You want to tell me about the other killings?" Stuart asked.

"Do I have to?"

"Yeah, Miles. It's sort of what makes you interesting to the general public."

"Shame, that, isn't it?

"Why victim two? Any particular reason?

"I worked for her years ago. She was a complete bastard. I can honestly say the world would be better off without her. Eventually, I took her out."

Stuart looked astonished. Miles made a slashing movement with his hand.

"No. *Took* her out."

"What... eh... What... was it like?"

"I don't have words for it, Stuart. A feeling of absolute power. A release from everything that makes you human or, at least, part of the human race. It's disgusting. Sickening. But... your head spins."

Miles' head was spinning right now and he felt sick. He sat up straighter and sucked hard, trying to coax more oxygen from the tank.

"You'd have to try it to understand."

"I don't appreciate comments like that. I really don't."

"Victim three? I'd never seen her before. Aw, there were a thousand pretty girls passing me by on the street every day. Too many women, Mozart. I was getting older. My hair was thinning. My time was ending. But I couldn't let it be over. Picking up dames was the only thing I'd ever been good at."

"Why didn't you just..." Stuart began. But Miles wasn't finished.

"I saw a woman. She was young, beautiful. She'd never look twice at me now. Never try to know me. So, I decided I would have her. I could do anything I wanted. Why not? Why the fuck not?"

"Cause... it's horrible, Miles."

"I know. That's why I killed her afterwards." Miles levelled a finger at Stuart. "See... anything is acceptable as long as you don't have to stare it in the face. Like when you ignore those starving people all over the world. Or the ones risking their lives to get to another country."

Miles summoned a last burst of energy.

"Death. Taxes. Your life slipping away. The shit this world is in. The pointlessness of it. Your pointless, shitty, mundane little life slipping away before your eyes. Anything at all. Don't you realise that? Anything is acceptable as long as you don't have to stare it in the face."

"No. No... no. I'm not taking that." Stuart shook his head. "I'm not taking that."

"Why? Cause it's not true or cause you don't fucking well want it to be true! If you're so squeamish, you're the wrong man for this job."

"I know the truth about you. You're a heartless killer."

"Simplistic! You realised that before you started! You were a struggling writer, just like me. And you jumped at the chance when I offered you the scoop of a lifetime. Believed me when I said I wouldn't harm you. That I'd show you where the bodies were."

"I wanted proof before I handed everything over to the police, you ass."

"I figured that. I didn't figure a fucking Great White was gonna tear your arm off on the way down to the wreck, then trap us here." Miles glanced at his watch. "I should be on my way to the bloody airport to catch a flight to the USA."

"I thought you might have contacted me because you secretly wanted to be caught. You'd have been tracked down if I'd survived. No matter where you went."

"I'm a master at hiding myself, remember? Maybe I just wanted to understand what it's like to be hunted. Give myself a scare, so I'd throw out the anchor a bit and get a grip."

Miles peered through the cabin windows. There was no sign of the shark and he assumed it had given up. He would have heaved a sigh of relief but couldn't spare the air.

"Let me ask you a question, Stuart." He decided to turn the tables. "Suppose there's someone you know and don't like. What stops you from killing them?"

"Some moral code, I guess."

"Would this be your own moral code?"

"Yes, it'd be my personal moral code."

Miles smiled thinly, ready to pounce.

"So, in that case... you could change your mind whenever it suited."

"Not at all," his companion protested. "I think we're also conditioned from childhood to adulthood, enforced with a decency the church or society, at one time or other, has put upon us."

"OK. Therefore, if you could get rid of the conditioning of church and society, your personal principles could be totally flexible. Wouldn't that follow?"

Stuart considered this before shaking his head.

"I think there is an atavistic fear in all of us about taking the life of someone else. We still subscribe to some arcane ideal we can't get rid of."

Miles leaned forward hungrily.

"Suppose you could take all the morals out of the world. Exorcise yourself from their hold. What would you replace them with?"

"Common decency?"

"That's a concept, Stu. Stop being coy."

"You'd replace them with the law of the jungle, I guess. Survival of the fittest."

"Dog eat dog." Miles shifted his gaze to the gauge. The tank was completely empty. "Thank you."

"Why don't you stop baiting me and fucking well ask them?" Stuart waved his good arm at the corpses. "You might get a different response."

One of the bodies lifted its head. The jaw was slack, held to the rest of the skull by a few loose tendons.

"My name is Jennifer Hillcross," it rasped. "I like typefaces and waltzing and drawing with fine art pens. I'd like to be richer; I'd like to be thinner. I used to live in Bundaberg but didn't like *that* much. I've got rats, three of them, though I don't keep them in a cage. They make me laugh. They do the funniest things. They were car sick last week because I moved to a new house. All three of them, holding onto the seat leather with their little claws."

She turned empty sockets towards Miles.

"I was looking forward to having my own place. I'd bought a new dress and was wearing it to a party when we met. Damn you to hell."

"I think this interview is over." Stuart sank onto his side.

"That's right. Cop out now!" Miles sucked as hard as he could, taking in one last lungful. "Where's the rule that says you can't do whatever you want? There's laws, sure, but why should you abide by a law if you don't want to? What if you don't want to do what other people tell you? There's no moral code out there in the ether everyone has to follow. There's no God and, even if there was, we don't have to obey him."

Both fists drummed on his knees.

"What did I do? Eh? Eh? I want to grasp what I did that was actually wrong!"

The other women began to crawl towards him, pieces of flesh drifting from their decaying, bitten bodies.

"I didn't know you!" Miles tried to push them back. "You mean as much to me as these starving kids I don't send money to help. Yes, I'm filled with self-loathing. Do I hate myself? Too right, I do. But I try to find some fucking *rule* to condemn myself and I can't find one! There's nothing to actually stop me!"

"It's the way the world works." Jennifer rasped, clawing at his leg. "That's what stops you."

"I don't like the way the world works!"

Miles inched away from the advancing women.

"We're just dogs slavering and straining at our collars. Pavlov's fucking dogs, that's what we are. And I slipped my leash! Broke away! Bad dog. Slap his nose! Slap all our noses when we shit or fuck or act in any way that's not deemed acceptable. Eh? When we do what we want to do but we're not allowed!"

He slid off the chair and shook his companion, releasing another plume of blood.

"Maybe that's what we need. Maybe we need *more* training, *more* conditioning. But, for Christ's sake, we need to be taught to show affection, not attack. How many times do rabid dogs like me have to turn on people? How many of us have to be put down before we decide to just stop breeding them?"

He kicked out at Stuart's motionless body, but his flippers got in the way and all he could manage was a penguin-like slap.

"Maybe you should have written a book about dog training." Stuart opened one eye. "You are remembering I'm dead, aren't you?"

"Of course," Miles grunted miserably. "Surprise, surprise. I'm trying to justify myself to myself. Me, me, me, eh?"

"No, you moron. It means I don't need my air tank anymore."

Miles goggled at him. Then he struggled out of his harness and clumsily swapped the man's scuba gear for his own. He switched masks and air from Stuart's cylinder flooded his lungs. Miles sat on the wooden floor for a while, breathing in sweet oxygen.

He looked around.

Tattered, chained bodies were scattered across the floor of the cabin, no longer moving. Miles swam to the window and looked out. He could see no sign of the predator. It had to have gone by now.

"Thanks, Stu. You've given me some much-needed perspective."

Miles still felt lightheaded but was refreshed enough to have a fair chance of reaching the surface. He shook Stuart's good hand, then let it drift away.

"I would have happily stuck to society's conventions, know that? But everybody twists them to suit themselves, so I ended up doing the same. Go big or go home, mate."

He opened the cabin door and cautiously ascended, recalling - just in time - to stop halfway up. It would be beyond ironic to get the bends this close to freedom.

Miles hung in the translucent water, watching the light filtering down from above. He had always loved diving. He was comforted by that sense of being cocooned and shut off from everything, alone in a silent, muffled world.

He was about to begin his journey again when the Great White emerged from the gloom. Must have measured 20 feet from tip to toe.

Miles tried to flee but was gripped by a terror more overpowering than anything he had ever experienced. He thrashed wildly but his arms and legs refused to comply. It felt like he was moving through soup.

"Please. Please, no! Don't hurt me!" he screamed. "I'm sorry! I'll do anything!"

The mask stopped any sound from escaping.

The creature opened its mouth, revealing two rows of vicious jagged teeth. It looked like it might be smiling, yet the blank, emotionless eyes were devoid of pity. It slowly moved towards him, a killing machine moulded by a million years of evolution. No rules. No compassion. No choices.

Miles continued to beg and plead, though he knew it would do no good.

"Ah," the shark said. "*Now*, you understand."

The Friendship Machine

All was quiet in the little town of Sewageboom. The only sound was the patter of raindrops, a cat wailing, the whistling of projectiles in flight, a grinding smash, several loud thumps, a dog barking, the rattle of machine gun fire and a sound like a giant elastic band hitting a trash can.

Harlan McFarlan glanced to the right and left and then above. Satisfied he was alone, he relaxed his karate stance and stood properly upright. He was wearing his usual gangster-style raincoat and had a plastic carrier bag on his head.

He stepped out of the shadows and into the menacing glare of the one unbroken streetlight. A wry smile touched his lips as he realised he had managed to walk all the way through Sewageboom without getting his hair wet. Or mugged. Or shot.

He halted at the doorway of *the Nipple Washers Arms* and ran his fingers fondly over teeth marks on the window sill. Then he stepped inside to find his client.

A few seconds later, he was back on the street, trying to untangle the door handle from his pocket. It came off in his hand, so he dropped it and continued indoors.

Memories flooded back. This was where his mother had met his father. Harlan Senior was employed as a living slot machine, while mum was president of the local biker chapter - *Satan's Chicken Slippers*.

Harlan had spent a happy childhood here. D ad would plonk him in the spittoon, out of harm's way, while his mum amused the boy by dropping her glass eye in his milk. Now, it was a sports bar with all the personality of Donald Trump's answering machine.

"Heh," Harlan grumped. "In my day, the dudes in here were so real they could fart the blues."

He spotted Fats skulking in a dark corner, nursing a pint of Guinness.

Harlan flicked a cigarette into his friend's drink to get his attention and waved to a group of scantily clad females, who completely ignored him. He plonked himself down opposite his companion with an odd sounding crunch.

"Don't sit on my pork crackles," Fats scowled.

"No sweat. Where did you put them?"

"Forget it."

"Don't just slouch about like a massive lounge lizard on a smooth jazz rock." Harlan glanced around. "You're supposed to give me the lowdown on the joint. That's what I'd be paying you for. If I was paying you."

"I came in an hour ago and asked a few subtle questions. But nobody had seen any strange faces."

"Except yours, of course," Harlan chuckled.

"Don't add to my self-esteem issues," Fats protested. "I hung around near the ladies' toilets for a while and even tried pumping the barman. He certainly seemed to like it."

"No clue as to who our client might be?" Harlan asked.

"I think the correct term is *whom*. That's an odd word, isn't it?"

"Get on with it, Fats."

"I did spot Louis the Tomahawk and Eddie the Beagle. They were having a dingo tickling contest in the back room."

"Louis and Eddie?" A look of alarm flashed across Harlan's face.

"I saw your girlfriend as well."

"Candy-Anne? I thought she'd moved away!" The look of alarm turned to one of panic and Harlan slid under the table.

"It's OK." Fats pulled him up by the ears. "I think she's unconscious."

"She's not my girlfriend anymore, buddy. She ditched me, remember?"

"And beat you senseless."

"Yeah. Let's not go there."

"Anyway, she came past, balancing four vodkas in each hand. She's a lovely girl, so I asked if you two were ever going to be an item again."

"What did she say?"

"She smashed a chair over my head."

"Wasn't in too bad a mood, then."

"Her eyes were crossed, so it was hard to tell." Fats pointed an accusing finger at him. "You broke her heart."

"And she broke my nose," Harlan sighed. "I swear she's not the girl I used to know."

"Oh, she is. I recognised her." Fats took a sip of his drink. "She told me if she saw you, she'd remove your unmentionables with a claw hammer."

"My unmentionables?"

"Yeah. So, I better not mention them. I think she's still mad about you always lying to her."

"I don't lie," Harlan huffed. "I just find truth a relative thing."

"True. And you can't pick your relatives. That's why friendship is so important."

Harlan stared at him in disbelief.

"Then she staggered off," Fats continued unperturbed. "Left me alone with my thoughts."

"That must have terrified them."

"When you're on your own in a bar, you get to thinking about metaphysical things. Like, what was the name of Kelly Maree's second single? Cause everyone remembers the first one, right?"

"Only if they're over 50 with a penchant for shit disco."

"Suddenly, Louis the Tomahawk was standing next to me, looking like a camel crapped in his window box." Fats twiddled his thumbs. "Then he reached down and grabbed hold of it."

"He *did*?"

"My Guinness. He picked the glass up, looked at it, put it down and walked away without a word. Why would he do that?"

"Perhaps he was trying to out-stare it."

"He's certainly not a man to be tinkled with but I decided to follow him anyway. He and Eddie the Beagle were going from table to table peering into the drinks.

"That's rather unhygienic."

"No. Peering. I stopped to take your girlfriend's head out of the ashtray. Hope I did right."

"Ex-girlfriend," Harlan repeated. "What happened next?"

"It just fell back in again."

"No! Louis and Eddie! What happened next?"

"Well, a really good song came on. It was one of my favourites… and this pretty little red-headed girl was smiling at me."

"Stop being so slap-happy and haberdash!" Harlan snapped. "Who and where is our client?"

"I don't know."

"Come on, mate. You talked to him on the phone!"

"But he didn't say anything except he'd be in here tonight wearing a pink orchid."

"How could you miss *that*?"

"Maybe he took it off. Would you wear a pink orchid in a rough joint like this?"

"It's not really my colour." Harlan tapped his friend's forehead. "Think, Fats. Isn't there anything else?"

"He did sound kind of foreign."

"Great. That means we're looking for someone who can dance in time to the music. Let's just keep our eyes open for something out of the ordinary."

"Candy-Anne is sitting upright and looking around. That count?"

Harlan slid under the table again.

"So she is." His muffled voice drifted up. "Something doesn't smell right, bud."

"That's probably my pork crackling, which you were squashing with your big hot ass."

"*Never* describe my ass as big and hot again." Seeing he was fairly safe in the shadowy booth, Harlan struggled back into his seat. "You know, I miss Candy-Anne, especially when she's wearing a skirt that short."

"It's a skirt?" Fats raised an eyebrow. "I thought it was a belt. You sure know a lot about women, Harlan."

"You've just got to see them as people." He leant over conspiratorially. "You see, Fats, girls are like cars."

"How so?"

"They weigh a lot."

He took off his coat and licked his lips.

"God, I need a drink. I'll go steal us some."

"Can't you just buy one?"

"I'm broke. Back in a mo."

He took off, keeping a wary eye out for Candy-Anne. Soon, sounds of violence erupted from the other side of the bar. Harlan returned carrying a tray of various beverages, including a large cocktail in a hurricane glass, a gaudy flower jostling with a paper umbrella for space on top.

"What an ordeal!" he panted. "I spotted one table where some hoons had just got up to dance. So I helped myself to their drinks. Then I noticed this interesting looking thing on top of the one armed bandit."

He indicated the cocktail.

"Anyhoo, I'd just picked it up and was about to return, mange tout, when Louis the Tomahawk and Eddie the Beagle appeared. Demanded I hand over the tray."

"What a nerve!" Fats was outraged. "They could have stolen their own. I hope you didn't stand for it."

"No. I was going to run. Then I decided to use my head instead."

"You nutted them?"

"I handed them the tray." Harlan looked smug. "See, I noticed a Nick Cave song had just come on.

"So everyone stopped dancing?"

"Correctamundo. The pisshounds returned to find Eddie and Louis holding their booze."

"Nice one! I take it a small fracas ensued."

"Medium rare. I obligingly took the tray back from Louis, as he needed both hands to hold on to his gonads."

"And you got out unscathed?"

"Absolutely. I smacked one bugger in the fist with my face and gave another several thumps in the knee with my nose." He wiped some blood from his lip. "They'll have a few scuff marks on their Nikes they won't forget in a hurry."

He slid a drink towards Fats.

"This one's yours. Half pint of Guinness, one Sambuca with pineapple and two Pickled Tinks. I put them all in the same glass for easy carrying."

"I don't normally mix my drinks," Fats admitted. "But it is Tuesday afternoon."

"This one's for me." Harlan reached for the cocktail. "I think it's a quadruple martini. You could use the umbrella in it to shelter from a typhoon."

He raised the drink to his lips.

"Get your hands *off* me!"

"Who said that?" Harlan looked around, puzzled.

"Listen, friend. Put your tongue near me again and you'll be wearing your tonsils on a string."

Harlan slammed the cocktail down and stared at it in horror. He reached out his hand experimentally.

"I'm warning you!"

"Oh my GOD!"

"Sorry to be rude," the cocktail said. "I get a bit abusive when someone tries to swallow me.

"Fats!" Harlan whispered. "My martini is talking to me!"

"I didn't know you'd had a falling out."

"Ha! Ha!" The cocktail gave a snort. "I like that. Nice going, pal."

"It's really talking to me." Harlan's eyes were on stalks. "I can't believe it."

"You *are* pretty anti-social."

"Dislikeable, even," the martini chipped in.

"I'm going to give up drinking."

"Now, that *is* hard to swallow," Fats sniggered.

"Well, I'm not, so paws off." The martini revolved on the table. "You must be Fats."

"Pleased to meet you." He shook the proffered straw. "And you are?"

"Call me Alan. Which one of you is Harlan?"

"I am, of course. The one who isn't Fats."

"Of course," Alan gave a hiccup. "It's a bit hard to focus."

"I suppose you haven't got eyes, have you?" Fats said sympathetically.

"It's not that," the cocktail replied. "I'm permanently pissed. Stands to reason, really."

"All right! All right." Harlan ran a hand down his face. "Let's stay calm about this."

"I'm calm as a newt."

"Me too." Fats took a huge gulp of his own concoction. "Drunk as well."

"Let me just check I'm not having a nightmare." Harlan began pinching his cheeks. "Wait a minute... How do you know our names?"

"I ought to," Alan scoffed. "I hired you."

"I knew I recognised your voice from somewhere," Fats slurred.

"God, I need a drink." Harlan reached out.

"Arghhhhhhhhhhhhhhhhhh!" the martini screamed.

"Arghhhhhhhhhhhhhhhhhhhh!" Harlan quickly withdrew his hand. "I'm sorry!"

"I just hope you don't make a habit of drinking your clients, is all."

"We don't know," Fats said. "Haven't had any for years."

"So, you've hired us, eh?" Harlan's shock was quickly replaced by a natural instinct to make money. "All right then, martini. Let's discuss payments."

"Oh, money's no object. I'll pay whatever you want."

"Good, that's exactly what we charge. Who do you want us to kill?"

"Nobody." Alan objected. "I want you to get me out of this place, first of all. There's a girl here and I don't like the way she keeps staring at me."

"Which one?

"Beats me. All human females look the same in the dark."

"Funny," Fats smiled. "That's what Harlan always says."

"I remember she kept falling off her stool and had her skirt on back to front."

"Candy-Anne!" Harlan looked nervously around.

"I'm not surprised she was staring at you," Fats commented. "She's an alcoholic."

"Aaaaaaaaaaaaaaargh! Don't let her get me."

"Shhhh. Shhhh," Harlan pulled Alan into an embrace. "She isn't an alcoholic. She just drinks more than most people."

"She drinks more than most neighbourhoods," Fats corrected.

"Harlan, I can't breathe."

"Apologies." He let the drink go.

"It's OK. I can't breathe any of the time."

"Let's continue this conversation somewhere else." Harlan shoved the martini towards his companion. "Fats? Put Alan under your coat and we'll blow the joint."

He gave a wry chuckle.

"I haven't sneaked a drink out of this bar since I was eight."

"You're not. I'm sneaking it out." Fats slid the martini into his jacket and weaved towards the door.

"We'll meet around the back," Harlan called. "Don't let the barman catch you."

"No worries, bud. Watch out for those hoons."

"What?" Harlan turned to find a dozen of Sewageboom's finest hard men advancing on him. "Ow! Ooyah, Ouch... Bloody hell... Oooh!"

Fats and Alan sat on upturned milk crates in a smelly side street, singing to each other.

Walk on. Walk on.

With hope in your hearts.

And you'll never walk aloooooooooooooooooone!

"You'll never walk at all, I guess." Fats gave his new friend a nudge.

"At least I can sing."

"Listen, do you know this one? *That's me in the spotliiiight...*"

The back door flew open and Harlan was catapulted into the alley. He pulled a pink blob from his mouth and threw it on the ground.

"Ha! You're not getting your nose back, neither."

He turned round and spotted his companions.

"There'll be a few higher-pitched voices in Sewage-boom tonight," he rasped, collapsing in a heap.

Fats ambled across and poured a drink over his partner's face.

"Come on, mate. Don't be a wimp."

Harlan put a hand to his face. Feeling wetness, he leapt to his feet, screaming.

"Get it off me! My God, it's eating my eyes!"

"Harlan, it's only Guinness."

"I'm over here," Alan waved his straw.

"Right, right." Harlan dusted himself off. "I think you better tell us why you hired Fats and me."

"I'm beginning to wonder that myself."

Before he could continue, Louis the Tomahawk and Eddie the Beagle appeared at the entrance to the alley, both carrying pool cues and a bag of tinnies.

"I think we'd like to hear that story too," Louis advanced on Alan. "You didn't tell me you knew Harlan."

"Me and him go back a long way, Louis," Alan grunted. "Several feet, at least."

"And you didn't tell us you knew Louis and Eddie," Harlan growled. "How *do* you know them?"

"That's simple enough," Eddie broke in. "We work for him."

"He hired us, too," Harlan grunted. "What are you playing at, you jumped up Cinzano?"

"Cinzano?" Alan turned purple. "How dare you insult me!

"Great," Harlan groaned. "Our client is a racist."

"If you got any dumber," Alan seethed. "You'd be an amoeba."

He spotted Eddie's puzzled look.

"That too big a word for you, Ed?"

"Amoeba is a *word*?"

"You don't have any reason to insult my pal," Louis warned.

"I know. I'm doing it for fun. Eddie the Beagle. What kind of stupid name is that?".

"About as stupid as a martini called Alan."

"Right!" the cocktail stammered. "You're fired."

"A belligerent drunk too." Harlan blew on his nails.

"You're fired as well! Go on. Beat it."

"Steady on, Alan," Fats cajoled. "Be reasonable."

"Bugger off. I don't need any of you."

"Suit yourself." They began to walk away.

"Waaaaaaaaaaaaaaah!" Alan burst into tears. "It's all right for you lot! You don't have to sit on a bar all day listening to the same Karaoke songs. You can walk down the street or scratch your nose when it gets itchy. I haven't even *got* a nose."

They trooped sheepishly back again.

"Don't cry," Louis pleaded. "I've got a nose you can have. I found it lying over there on the ground."

He stuck the pink lump on the side of the glass using a wad of chewing gum.

"You don't know what it's like," Alan sniffed, trying out his new shnozz. "Always looking at the world through the bottom of a glass."

"Can't you see through the sides?"

"I guess I'd better explain why we're all here," Alan pulled himself together. "Hadn't I?"

"Yes, you better."

"I hired Harlan and Fats to do something for me."

"Fix you up with a nice little lime?"

"I wanted them to get me off this planet."

"That's understandable." Harlan shrugged. "Fats, how high can you throw?"

"I'm serious!" Alan shouted. "Surely it occurred to you that I'm not actually a talking fucking drink?"

They all looked at each other.

"Nope."

"I'm an alien, you morons. I just happen to look like a martini."

"That's the most ridiculous thing I ever heard," Louis snorted.

"I thought if I hired Harlan and Fats, they could help me get off earth. They came highly recommended."

"OK. *That's* the most ridiculous thing I ever heard."

"Don't rule us out because we're incompetent." Harlan frowned. "If you employed us to get you off the planet, Alan, what did you hire *those* goons for?"

"Bodyguards."

"Bodyguards? I wouldn't use them as mudguards."

"Hey!" Eddie protested. "We may hate violence, but we're good at it. That's why we tried to jump you earlier. We were alarmed about you abducting Alan."

"Nice bit of alliteration, Ed." Louis nodded appreciatively.

"I don't think that's a word either, but thanks."

"I understand." Fats stroked the cocktail's dewy side soothingly. "Half of that bar would kill their own granny for a drink."

His eyes widened.

"Hello, Candy-Anne. How long have you been listening?"

"Long enough." The woman stepped out of the shadows. "Louis, Eddie, Fats. How's it hanging?"

"Hey, doll," Louis replied nervously. "Good to see you standing."

"Harlan." Her eyes narrowed.

"Hi, babe." He shuffled around on the spot until Candy-Anne turned her attention to Alan.

"You must be the talking drink, huh?"

"No, I'm Ron De Santos."

"Sorry for staring earlier but you certainly are well proportioned."

"Hands off, Betty. Got my homies protecting me."

Candy-Anne moved toward the martini. Louis blocked her path. She kneed him in the groin and he sank to his knees.

"Don't worry, Lou." Eddie patted his head. "You never needed your knacks much, anyway."

"Relax, Al." She winked. "Cocktails are for pussies. I like shots."

"That lot aren't going to be able to help me, are they?" Alan heaved a huge sigh.

"I seriously doubt it," Candy-Anne admitted. "Harlan's the smartest one and he's still an idiot."

"I'm not standing round here just to be insulted," Harlan huffed.

"Where do you usually go?" Alan gave a guffaw. "Sorry. That's a bar joke. I hear a lot of them."

He adopted a cajoling tone.

"Since you're all here, let's party a little. There's lots of booze, though I hate to say it. Shame to waste good liquor, eh?"

"That's true," Harlan relented. "What about it, Louis?"

"My swollen gonads say no." Louis struggled into a sitting position. "But my tongue says yes."

"I've used that line!" Harlan grinned.

"*Seriously*?" Candy-Anne glared at him and he winced.

"This is what I like about earth," Alan chuckled. "It's got atmosphere. That's another bar joke."

"What the hell." Candy-Anne emptied out the bag of tinnies and everyone helped themselves. For a while, they drank in silence, eyeing each other suspiciously.

"Well, this is pleasant." Fats raised his can in salute. "It's the first time in years we've all been together without arguing."

"We've done nothing but argue," Harlan pointed out.

"Not at this precise moment, though."

"We are now."

"We're not. We're discussing."

"All right! I don't want to argue with you."

"Guys, guys!" Alan interrupted. "Stop it. Looks like you used to be friends. So, what happened?"

"Nothing. Time passed.

"Come on. I wasn't uncorked yesterday. What is it with you lot?"

"I don't want to bore you," Harlan grunted.

"Yes, he does. It's his specialty."

"I won't be bored," Alan insisted.

"Yes, you will." Eddie stroked his exceedingly large chin. "But here goes. Eh... I guess the natural inhibitions of small-town society, mixed with a clash of Alpha male egos, worked as a repressing agent and created a pushing away effect which turned to resentment."

"That and the fact Harlan stole my car," Louis added.

"Tell him the truth, guys," Candy-Anne threatened.

The former companions looked at each other.

"At one time, we ran a detective agency together," Harlan said. "The Sewageboom Panthers. Candy-Anne was our secretary."

"Despite being more competent than the rest of them put together."

"We were young, enthusiastic and absolute bastards, so reckoned we could go far. We had a modest little office in Eddie's toilet."

"Embarrassed even."

"Our leader was a bloke called Big Dick McShane."

"Truly unfortunate handle," Alan whistled. "Where is *he*?"

"That's the sad part." Fats took up the story. "One day, we were approached by a bunch of bedraggled villagers. Their hamlet was being terrorised by a gang of vicious bikers, so the town scraped together their possessions and asked for our help. Said we were their last hope."

"Why didn't they go to the police?" Alan inquired.

The others burst out laughing.

"Fair enough. What did you do?"

"We told them to get lost."

"All except Big Dick," Harlan sipped his drink sadly. "He persuaded us to go and protect them."

"Just the five of you?"

"He was counting on recruiting some villagers when we got there. But there was a flaw in that plan."

"Yeah. If they'd intended to fight, they wouldn't have hired us in the first place."

"The women were all called Calum," Eddie complained.

"Anyway, we taught them the meagre defence techniques we knew, like screaming and hiding. Built some adobe walls. Then we settled down to wait."

"For three months," Louis recalled bitterly. "I've never been so bored."

"Yet they still took you by surprise," Candy-Anne snorted.

"They came on a Sunday afternoon!"

"They were bikers, not Jehovah's Witnesses."

"Next thing anyone knew, we were locked in mortal combat," Fats continued. "Many a villager was injured running into lampposts or tripping over crisp packets."

"Still, we fought nobly for at least 8 minutes," Eddie said proudly. "Except Harlan."

"I was under Louis' car, considering the best course of action."

"Which turned out to be driving off in it."

"*You* jumped into a passing truck carrying nuclear waste." Harlan jerked a thumb at Louis. "They finally dumped him in the Coral Sea. He still glows in the dark."

"I spent two years in a cave," Louis shuddered. "Hiding from men with Geiger counters."

"Eddie surrendered and joined the bikers as a navigator," Fats said. "They ended up in the Coral Sea as well."

"I saved the village, didn't I? And where were you?"

"In the toilet," Fats replied sheepishly. "I've got a weak bladder."

"There you have it. We all betrayed each other and haven't been pals since."

"What about Big Dick?" Alan was certainly an attentive listener.

"He buggered off too. We didn't expect that."

"He didn't run out," Candy-Anne corrected. "How many times do I have to tell you? A huge flying saucer appeared on top of the hill and sucked him up."

"Do you honestly expect us to believe Dick was sucked off by aliens?"

"Sucked *up*."

"By aliens!" Louis scoffed. "A likely st..."

His voice trailed off and he slowly turned to look at the martini.

"Ehhh. Alan? Why exactly *did* you hire us?"

"Some bloke in a bar had one of your business cards. Suggested you'd be the very people to help me out."

"Where was this?"

"Cirrus 5. In the Horseshoe Nebula."

"Was it *Dick*?"

Alan thought for a moment.

"Did he have four arms?"

"Don't think so. He always had the right number of sleeves."

"That was him, then. Everyone else in the pub was a double quadruped."

"Do you know what this means?" Fats was the first to catch on. "Big Dick is up there somewhere, still running a detective agency."

"I believe we owe you an apology, Candy-Anne," Louis said contritely.

"And six months back pay." She shrugged. "Still, I think it's time we let bygones be bygones. Group hug?"

"Nope."

"Not a chance."

"When hell freezes over."

"C'mon guys," Candy-Anne pleaded. "Would it really hurt that much?"

"Hmmm. I suppose not."

As they moved together, arms outstretched, Harlan kneed Louis in the groin.

"That's for being a big beardy bumhole."

"Ooooh," Louis wheezed. "It hurt after all."

"You ok?" Eddie helped him to his feet.

"Not in the slightest."

"Good." Eddie kneed him in the balls as well. "I love this game."

Louis straightened up and punched both of them in the mouth.

"I am going to fucking kill you and then shit in your cremation urns."

They rolled across the dirty alley floor, slapping and kicking each other. While they were distracted, Candy-Anne shuffled closer to Fats and slid something into his pocket. Then she quickly dropped a pill into Alan's glass.

There was a loud parping from the tangle of bodies.

"Oh no! Someone did a fluffy!"

"Christ! That fart stinks of sweaty, rancid bum crack."

They broke apart, still swiping at each other.

"Can we get back to the business at hand?" Alan interrupted. "I need you to build me a matter transmitter ASAP so I can get out of this hellhole."

"Sounds pretty technical," Harlan straightened his collar. "I have trouble with Lego."

"I'm serious. You get me the materials and I'll show you how to make it."

"It might not be easy getting parts," Fats said. "Sewageboom only has Foodworks, a post office and 24 pubs."

"The main component is spaghetti."

"I could handle that. Short or long cut?"

"Doesn't matter. You could ditch those losers and come with me if you wanted. Have you ever seen the seven moons of Cagliostro?"

"I don't go to the movies much."

"You might find Big Dick there."

"You could have phrased that a little better," Fats blanched. "But it's a tempting offer."

"I think this cruel practical joke has gone on long enough." Candy-Anne leaned over and pulled a book from Fats' pocket.

"I thought so." She held up the cover for them to see. "*Advanced Ventriloquism.*"

The others stared at him.

"Fats? Are you making that martini talk?"

"It's not my book! Alan… say something!"

There was no sound from the cocktail.

"Eddie?" Louis held out his hand. "Pool cue, please."

"Shit!" Fats turned and ran with Louis and Eddie in hot pursuit.

"Aw, Fats," Harlan sighed. "I never figured you'd do something so underhand. That's my role."

"He runs fast for a ventriloquist." Louis and Eddie trotted back. "Well, we better head. Give us your number, Harlan. We'll have a catch-up sometime."

"2556452131." Harlan lied. Neither wrote it down.

"Nice to see you again, Candy-Anne." Eddie bent to kiss her hand and she poked him in the eye.

"Too soon. Got it."

He and Lois backed away and vanished.

Harlan hung around for a moment before plucking up the courage to speak.

"I best be off too, Candy-Anne. You... eh... want to go for a drink sometime?"

"No."

"OK. Yup. Take care."

He shuffled into the night.

Candy-Anne took a tubular object from her bag and pointed it at Alan. It bleeped twice.

"Oooh. What happened? Did you just *roofie* me?"

"I'm here to take you back. Hope you don't intend putting up a fight."

"What am I going to do? Fire straws at you?"

"We both know you're capable of much more than that. You can't hurt me, though."

She didn't notice Fats sneak back into the alley.

"*I* can." He pointed a gun at her through his coat pocket. "So, I better get some explanations fast."

"*I'll* tell you the whole story," Alan urged. "Kill her first."

"You both better spill. I'm out of breath, fucked off my tits and everyone hates me. I'm starting to get pretty ratty."

"The truth is a bit implausible," Alan warned.

"Says the talking martini." Fats sat on an upturned crate. "Candy-Anne? What's going on?"

"There are huge similarities in all the races across the galaxy." The girl took a deep breath and sat down next to him. "Everyone has the same problems and worries."

"You mean there's a whole universe full of depressed people out there?"

"Pretty much."

"*That's* depressing."

"This… object is supposed to help." She indicated Alan. "He's a Mass Anxiety Reversal Therapy Internal Negation Integer. MARTINI for short."

"I'm getting a bad feeling," Fats sighed.

"Martinis are designed to sit in pubs and listen to people's struggles," Candy-Anne continued. "That's why Alan looks the way he does. All inhabited planets have bars, you see."

"Thank God for that."

"The setup is much the same as here. Except women can go in on their own without getting harassed."

"Just tell the story."

"Martinis are programmed to cheer them up. Get everyone talking to each other. Friendship machines if you like. Except, it doesn't always work."

"And then?"

"If they can't fix the problems, they scoot out some euphoric gas to make everyone forget their troubles for a while."

Fats gave Alan a nudge.

"So, your job is to make any world a better place?"

"That's right."

"Doesn't sound so bad, CA."

"Problem is, this one went rogue. Alan would show the customers how to make a matter transmitter, promising guaranteed happiness in return. Then he'd transport himself to another planet. But not before he overdosed them, leaving behind a bar full of zombies with their minds completely wiped."

"Why would you do that, buddy?" Fats frowned.

"People fuck me off. They wander in, get pissed and talk about the things they're going to do and how their lives are going to be different. I listen. I encourage them. Off they go. Next night, they're back and I have to do the same thing all over again. Six months of that nonsense almost sobered me up."

"Sounds a bit like the *Nipple Washers Arms*." Fats stroked his chin. "Where did you learn *how* to make something like that? I meant to ask."

"You pick up a lot hanging around bars."

"True. That's where Harlan picked up Candy-Anne.

"When it was done," Alan said. "I'd transport myself somewhere else, sure. But I always kept my side of the bargain."

"You zombify whole pubs," Candy-Anne snarled.

"I only gas people if I can't make them satisfied any other way. And, you have to admit, they're blissfully happy. Don't even drink anymore."

"Plus, it was pretty handy for covering your trail."

"Got any left?" Fats inquired.

"Fats!"

"Sorry." He prodded his human companion. "What's this all got to do with you, CA?"

"Big Dick McShane was hired to hunt Alan down. But, instead of arresting him, he suggested *the Nipple Washers Arms* as a great next destination and recommended the Sewageboom Panthers as the perfect people to help him."

"We've never been recommended before," Fats blushed. "Though I *was* once followed home by a flasher."

"Dick contacted me and offered to split the reward money. All I had to do was wait around in the pub for Alan to appear."

"I guess it wasn't much fun for you."

"Not until I discovered pineapple vodka."

"Hah," Alan interrupted. "She wouldn't know how to have fun if she was on fire. I still think you should shoot her."

"Why didn't Big Dick apprehend Alan right away?" Fats stuck out his lip. "Why didn't you grab him the moment you saw him? Why go through this charade and make me look like a liar?"

"Despite all appearances, I got to quite like Louis and Eddie. Even Harlan. And Dick was their mentor. He hated the way they all turned on each other."

"I don't get it."

"The martini is programmed to help people. Bring them together." Candy-Anne shrugged. "We wanted to give Alan a chance to actually make you friends again."

"But you sabotaged that!"

"They were kicking seven bells out of each other! In another minute Alan was going to start gassing the place. He wouldn't be able to help himself."

"True dat," Alan agreed. "If only to cover up that smelly fart."

"I had no choice but to get rid of you lot and neutralise him." Candy-Anne squared her shoulders. "You still gonna shoot me?"

"This isn't a gun." Fats lowered his hand. "It's a door handle."

"Looks like the party's over," Alan said sadly.

"Don't be mad at me, buddy."

"You did what you had to do. I'm an illegal alien."

"I'll kind of miss you, Alan."

"Let's go, martini." Candy-Anne waved the cylinder in the air and a glowing blue portal appeared.

"OK. Remember, you're driving."

"Shaken but not stirred, eh? Don't worry, I've had four coffees."

"Fair enough. Bye Fats. You can have my umbrella."

"It's not raining."

"Good job. It's made of paper."

Candy-Anne picked up the martini and stepped through the portal. It closed with a small raspberry sound.

Fats sat on the ground and lit a cigarette. Picking up Alan's discarded nose, he stared at it miserably.

"Hey, buddy." A voice whispered behind him. "You can pick your friends but you can't pick your friend's nose."

"Harlan!" Fats spun round. "You came back!"

"Once I thought about it, I realised you'd never pull a fast one like that. You're too decent a guy." Harlan ruffled his companion's hair. Fancy a drink?"

"I think I'll stick to Coke from now on."

"*Really*?"

"Yeah," Fats grinned. "But put a bit of rum in it."

The March of the Eligible Bachelorettes

History repeats itself only in that, from afar, we all seem to lead exactly the same life.

We are all born; we all spend time here on earth; we all die. But up close, we have each walked down our own separate paths. We have stood at our own lonely crossroads. We have touched the lives of others at crucial points, for better or for worse. In the end, each of us has lived a unique life story, astounding and complicated, a story that could never be repeated.

Edward Bloor

"I wouldn't ask too much of her," I ventured. "You can't repeat the past."

"Can't repeat the past?" he cried incredulously. "Why of course you can!"

He looked around him wildly, as if the past were lurking here...

F Scott Fitzgerald. The Great Gatsby

Yesterfield 2023

It is autumn.

Swirls of yellow leaves dance in the grass hollows above the beach. They settle and rise with each gust of the biting wind, half-forgotten memories that will not stay buried. He kicks through one pile, enjoying the swish of his make-believe sacrilege. A cloud of bug-filled dust rises around him and he retreats to the play park, patting at his jeans as he sits on a swing. In the distance, a porcupine ridge of swaying masts and rigging announces the fishing fleet has returned to harbour – a reminder that not everyone sails for pleasure or to reach far-flung places.

The breeze picks up and chains creak softly around him. Even seats that are deserted join in. The roundabout is turning slowly as if he has just missed children at play. He lights a cigarette, shielding the flame with his hand.

Yesterfield 1981

Jenny

How's life? I'm in sec studies just now but all I do is sit and stare out the window. I fancy you like fuck. I wish you'd chuck Joanne so I can go out with you. Why should you like Joanne better? You never said you did, anyway. I think about you most at school and at night times. I know I'm only 16, but I can still go out with boys that are 19.

I spend whole afternoons sitting with Frankie in Visocchi's café under the shabby candy-striped awning. Neither of us ever say anything to each other so we must be comfortable with it. Or we couldn't strike up a proper conversation if our lives depended on it. I mean there's only the two of us. But he's always there and so am I.

We smoke John Player Specials, wear leather jackets and our earrings are in the left lobes. Frankie has streaked hair too - but that's more a fashion mistake than a rebellious statement. The other customers stare at us disapprovingly.

"What?" I say, not looking them in the eye. "Yobs will be yobs."

Out the seccy hut window I can see the school playing fields. I can see an old woman walking along the sand with a wiggly bum. I can see the distant lighthouse. I can see too bloody much.

"Crash the ash, Mrs Smoker," Frankie says. And he starts singing.

"Hello hello hello... this is the lord God, can you hear? Hellfire and damnation's what I've got for you down here."

For two minutes I can't stop thinking about you. I think I fell in love the minute I set eyes on you. Will you be in the Den when I get out at 4.00pm? If you say no to going out with me, I'd still like to be your friend.

Crooky comes in.
"Fit like, wankers?"
"Hello, Mrs Smoker."
Crooky flicks his fingers in front of Frankie's eyes to see if he's been taking magic mushrooms. In magic mushroom season, Frankie has a permanent crick in his back from walking bent over.

Joanne
Hey! When I asked what you and Frankie were doing crawling round Middlefield Park you told me you were looking for a contact lens.

Didn't know if you'd be shocked.

You remember when me and you went to Lucy's house to watch Salem's Lot on TV? Tracy and Jimmy Boyd got together and so did Lucy and Darren Ogden even though she's posh and he's fat. It was that kind of night. Lucy's parents were out, so after the film finished, she left the lights off. That was the first time you touched me properly. You put your hand up my jumper.

How could I forget?

I grabbed your wrist then I moved it somewhere more... intimate. I couldn't see your face in the dark but I'm pretty sure it was shocked.

Touché.

Yeah. You obviously didn't need to speak sexy and French to get what I wanted.

On the way home Joanne and I sit in the play park by the beach, with the stone train and the swings and roundabout. And the empty paddling pool. It's just as dark down here, though a thousand stars graffiti the night sky and gulls are screaming wraiths playing cosmic join the dots. Freezing too, but that doesn't stop us. The thrill of being discovered is replaced by a more natural excitement. Besides, under that vast canopy — with the endless, timeless sea crashing over the shore - we feel too small for youthful indiscretions to matter. We talk for about two hours before I walk you home.

I didn't notice until bedtime that my tights now had seams up the front.

Why did the chicken cross the road?

Don't know.

To apply for its old age pension. You get it?

"Yes... hah, hah hah!" I tried to act cool like I was in on the joke. You just looked puzzled.

The chicken didn't.

I kissed you goodnight and went in and made some toast. You don't like eating toast in my house because there's always dog hair stuck to it. I looked out the window and could see the end of your cigarette glowing in the dark at the end of my street. It occurred to me that you were shortening your life so I knew where you were. You probably just got cold.

She opens the back door to let her dog out and waves from inside the shaft of light.

My mum likes you. She thinks you have nice hair. I went to the Thistle Club last night but it was no fun without you. Frankie wants to get off with me. He isn't going to. And, of course, they played Ant Music. I went to bed with the little stuffed panda you gave me.

I meet Joanne on the rebound from Emma. Emma chucked me for snogging Fiona Finlay. Fiona was Bill McCombie's girl, even though he was sneaking about with Carol Conner. Emma was sarcastic with a wonderful laugh and Psoriasis covered both ears until, eventually, they fell off. Well, her earrings did. Ripped right through the lobes, leaving two track marks like she was part of some exotic tribe. She wore scarlet straight-leg jeans over tights, white stilettos and her mother had an ashtray that belonged to Hitler. Or so she claimed. Emma got My Guy and Photo-Love magazines delivered every week, so I'd come around on Saturday mornings and read them. Everyone thought she was hard as nails but she just had that kind of face.

She was my first proper girlfriend and I was crazy about her.

Emma

You know one way or another you'll come back and get me. We'll end up together in ten years, cause you never forget your first love. I'll meet you in ten years.

I try to forget her by sitting on a summer seat. A magpie watching the schoolgirls flocking along the esplanade, catching their shiny, precious glances. Girls that live in the country leave the car park on rust-flecked buses and can't come back at night to hang around the shorefront. Town girls are more sophisticated, anyway. Country girls are bred to pull ploughs if their dad's tractor breaks down.

Short skirts have been banned by the headmaster, Mr Elder, so the girls have to establish their independence some other way. Buttons unfastened to the waist.

Lipstick applied in the toilets and removed at garden gates. The March of the Eligible Bachelorettes, I call it. Surf crashes behind them and the sea glitters like a jewelled carpet - but they are louder and more eye-catching.

Job done.

I haven't seen you in ages. There's an appropriate song on the radio. 'Special Brew' by Bad Manners - and the lyrics, I think, are about me and you.

'I don't care, when they stare, at the way that I'm always with you.

We're a pair, it's not fair when they say we're a special brew'.

I'm really sorry we split up now. I didn't realise how much I'd miss you. I enjoyed Friday. The Tannadice disco was great fun, probably because I was sloshed, pished and drunk.

Tannadice disco's where I first see Joanne. Then I meet her again at Northfield Youth Club when me and Frankie and Ed go up the youth club to play pool. Well, Ed goes to play pool. Me and Frankie go to check out the talent.

Hopefully I'll meet you on Monday. I hope you realise how much I love you. Please, please meet me on Monday behind the health centre after school and we can go sit on the swings and talk. If you can.

I fancy Tracy, really. Paul Morrison said he'd felt her tits in the school cloakroom and she hadn't even had them very long. Tracy is small, dark and sort of... elfin. Joanne is small, blonde and sort of elfin too. In fact, Lucy is quite elfin as well. But she's tall and elves should have some sort of height limit.

Tracy plays four games of pool with me and I ask her out to the Kingoldrum disco. Well... I ask if she's going and she says aye and she asks if I'm going, so I say aye as well. It's all in the ayes. Frankie says he would definitely stick it in her ear and shout sherbert.

The Kingoldrum disco is in a country hall with a mud-paved drive out front and back road rutted by tractor tracks. Everyone makes their own way to it and back, which is the way with most things in life.

Hilly arrives on his yellow Kawasaki. Me and Ed try to hitch a lift from Yesterfield Boulevard. Lads are always cruising around there in grey Ford Cortinas, like sharks with acne, hoping to pick up someone who has missed the organised bus and doesn't look like the back of one. We have no luck.

The organised bus quickly turns into a mobile pub - a human Noah's ark with all the liquid inside. Girls share vodka and gin in paper cups. Paul Morrison manages to climb all the way into the luggage rack and sticks his tadger through the mesh.

Joanne

I came up on the Kingoldrum bus with Lucy and Gwen. We drank half a bottle of vodka and some unidentified liquid Lucy nicked from her parents' booze cabinet. Peem Wilson's Vauxhall Viva got stuck behind us and we could see June in the passenger seat, like she always was, holding a can of Tennent's Super Lager. There was usually a green plastic strip with Peem and June written on it, stuck across the top of the windscreen. But Ed had unsuccessfully tried to rip it off for a laugh and now it just said '...m and June.'

The crowd in the back seat started hugging each other, making kissy faces and chanting "mmmm and June, mmmm and June." Frankie flashed his arse at them and somebody stuck a cigarette in it.

Hey Joanne. You seen Tracy?

She couldn't make it. Emma isn't here either, in case you're wondering.

Really? Suppose I'll have to talk to you then, eh?

Suppose you will.

In the hall, I try to impress Joanne by making fun of my friends.
"That's Ed dancing over there." Ed's corn-coloured hair flaps up and down. "The one that looks like

he's trying to dislodge a parrot from each shoulder without using his hands."

Joanne giggles and I am encouraged.

"Who's that?"

"Eh? That's Frankie."

"He looks like he's running on the spot." I'd gotten the hang of the game.

It's the "I-have-just-seen-a-UFO school of boogie." Frankie is lit up by a disco ball right above. Because he's on mushies, it transfixes him. "See the guy whose dancing bears no resemblance to the music?" I point to one head bobbing well above the rest. "That's Hilly."

Joanne laughs again.

"Dancing bears," I said. "It would make a good name for a band."

At the end of the night came the slow songs. I was never able to remember the first one we danced to. Might have been 'Baby, I Love You' by the Ramones...

Joanne gets back on the bus when the hall empties and Frankie climbs on the back of Hilly's bike for a dice with death. I leave the hall with Ed and we walk down the black leafy tunnel, away from Kingoldrum's lights. We know someone will pick us up. That's the whole point of the Kingoldrum disco. Picking people up.

"I thought you liked Tracy." Ed kicks a can down the road. "But it looks like you scored with Joanne. Yum, yum."

"Yup. At least I got my elf."

"What?"

"You don't get it?"

Ed doesn't get it.

Emma

I couldn't make it to Kingoldrum cause I was grounded by my parents. Mr Elder was walking along the esplanade, saw me smoking and told me to put it out.

"What time is it?" I asked.

"Four-thirty."

"What time does school finish?"

"Four o'clock."

"Then fuck off."

Frankie and I sit in Vissocchi's. Crooky has gone home to watch Danger Mouse. *I could go home too but the one day I do a flying saucer will land in the town square. Frankie starts singing.*

"Flying saucer attack. I'm never coming back. Oh, oh, oh, once till it's over."

Monday afternoon. grey skies. Half day. Everything closed.

Jenny

I go through the Den on my way home from school. That way, if I meet you, Joanne won't be able to see us. Nobody will. It's quiet here and the air is filled with insects.

The Den is a small green valley in a small seaside town and the Sunday school picnic was invented to fill it.

But most days you're in Visocchi's when the school comes out.

The monument on the esplanade looks like some grimy workman's finger. It annoys the clouds. You can't see the town clock from the back of Visocchi's but that's okay, cause it doesn't work. You can tell when it's 4.00 because a herd of schoolgirls start to pass the window and some drift through the door. Bridget Visocchi shuffles past. A long, striped apron swathes her body but we know by the way she walks that she has no legs. Just really long hips that extend right down to her feet. Or castors, like a well upholstered couch.

"Getta you feet down offa da seat!"

What, Eh? Frankie? What did she say?

Emma

It's ten past four. Maybe you couldn't make it. Maybe I was inside the health centre when you came past. I suppose I can give it a few more minutes.

Frankie slams his feet down but misses all three of Bridget's Pomeranians because they're smarter than him. Poor Bridget. Her prices are too high but it doesn't matter. Nobody ever buys anything. Crooky can make one hot Ribena last five hours.
"Goodbye Mrs Smoker," Frankie says.
Bridget grunts and waddles into the back.

Joanne

I won't be able to see you in Visocchi's at four today. Now that I know I got into Stirling Uni, I have to talk to my mum and dad about grants and stuff.

No sign of Joanne. But in come the schoolgirls, startling the door chimes. Bridget still hasn't noticed the Tampon Bunch hung up there yesterday. In comes Young Div and Young Doob and Helen with the mole, and wee Alison who doesn't love me anymore. In comes Fraz's girlfriend, Shirley with the big passionate head. In comes Jingles with the bells on her fringed white boots. The Young Mental Shade pile in and climb

over the front seats, like stormtroopers into a tank.
Frankie throws matches at them.

Still no Joanne.

Right. Fuck this. I'm off, Frankie.

Emma

I see you run past the health centre and jump the low wall into the Den. I don't shout but, on impulse, I follow you.

Jenny

I see you walking along the floor of the Den. No Joanne. Brilliant.

Joanne

I see you from the ridge on the other side of the Den as I'm turning off for my house. I'm sure that's Jennifer Sim on the path above you. From this angle, it looks like she's standing on your head. Like you're acrobats trying some dangerous act for the first time, out of sight of the public.

That end of the Den narrows and thickens seductively. The foliage is dense. The smell is damp and musty. It's the way to Jenny's house.

Further in there is an old fly-blown iron bridge,
where Emma and I used to hold hands and spit into the
water.

Emma

I see you sitting in the playpark. It's not as good as the one on the boulevard but it's much quieter so I understand why you're there. I spot Jenny Sim watching you. Back and forward you swing, showing off how high you can get.

Showing off for her.

Joanne

Desperately trying to fly and getting nowhere. I'll miss you though.

Emma

I'm going home. I've got to get out of this damned town. You never forget your first love but it doesn't make them any less of a dick.

Jenny

I should just go down there. It's only a few short steps. Say "fuck it" and go down and sit on your knee and kiss you.

But I'm too scared.

Yesterfield 2023

"Hey, pal!" A teenage girl is watching him. "You not a bit old to be sitting on swings?"

She has thick black eyeliner and baggy black jeans covered in straps and buckles. She looks a bit like the punk rockers of old. Yet it's still a small town, after all, so she's wearing trainers because there's nowhere to buy proper chunky boots.

"I was waiting for someone." The man flicks his cigarette expertly into the bushes. "But I don't think she's coming."

The girl looks disinterestedly at her watch.

"When were you meant to meet her?"

The man puts his feet on the ground and stops the swing. Motionless, he is still vaguely handsome but his hair is thinning and his features lined and rather pasty.

"1981."

The girl isn't listening. She has spotted a long-haired boy at the other end of the esplanade and runs towards him, waving. Her strappy black trousers flap like the wings of a gull and she screeches a welcome in much the same fashion.

"Kids," the man says without a trace of emotion.

And then, she's there. She wears a long suede coat and matching gloves. Her leather boots look both foreign and expensive.

"Hey, stranger." She sits down next to him. "Never thought I'd hear from you again."

"Didn't expect you to answer my email." A big, stupid grin splits his face. She remembers it well. He glances sideways at her.

"You look good." It's true, though he's astonished to see her hair is pure white.

"I know."

"Been following you on Facebook. You've done well." He looks around. "Why did you pick here of all places?"

The petrels scream in indignation, hovering over the car park where Visocchi's used to stand.

"Only bit I still recognise. I hear the Den's a housing estate now." She shrugs. "What would you like to do?"

The sea crashes on the rocks. He takes a deep breath and bites his lip. Pats his knees nervously. It reminds her of a lost child and what he says next only reinforces that.

"I suppose starting again is out of the question?" he jokes.

She laughs, despite herself. They are not the same people and no longer know each other, if they ever did. Have no idea what real triumphs or damage the years have visited, so the question is bold and quaint and careless and silly. All the things she liked about him and all the things she didn't.

"Fuck it." She gets up and he makes to rise too, unsure of how to act. With a shake of the head, she straddles him and kisses him on the lips.

"Holy shit." He looks shocked and delighted.

She is shocked and delighted too — not just by his reaction but her own daring. For a long time she has felt like a shadow of her former self and senses he is the same. The sun breaks briefly through the clouds and the light is bright and unforgiving, illuminating every line. Yet, they last met when they were both young and, in some small way, it's how they'll always see each other. Knowing this, Yesterfield transforms into a place of possibilities rather than a prison. Age becomes experience. Life is an adventure. The past moves closer and the future recedes.

It's never too late to keep an unfulfilled promise, she thinks.

"A stroll down memory lane is a lot more exciting when you and I are the only familiar landmarks." She struggles up and pats his cheek. "Fancy a walk?"

"Christ, you make me feel like a teenager again," he laughs. "Are we going to hold hands?"

"I'll consider it." She pulls him to his feet and winks. "Wouldn't want to rush things, though, would we?"

The Mechanical Bull

Once upon a time, there were three brothers who ran a building yard in Ipswich. Everyone complained they were cowboys, so they decided they'd better act the part, not wanting to disappoint their customers. Business was brisk, for whenever the trio ran out of work, they'd drive around in a pickup truck - breaking windows and knocking down lampposts. Their names were Wiggly, Bob and Fugly Mutterfunk, and they had a young stepbrother called Boring Norman, because his job was drilling holes in planks. At least, that's what they told him.

Then, one day, the annual Line Dance and Rodeo came to town. Wiggly read about it in the local paper, which he had borrowed from his next door neighbour's letterbox. He also borrowed the letterbox, so he could come over and fix it when his neighbour grumbled about the draught.

"Says here there's a prize of a wooden Koala for the person who can stay on a mechanical bull longest!" he roared. "Bet I can win that!"

"And just how do you figure to beat me?" Bob retorted. "I'll be entering, too."

"I'm gonna superglue my bum to the saddle." Wiggly pulled an economy-sized tube of adhesive from inside his trousers, where he kept it to impress the checkout girls at Coles.

"Darn! That's pretty clever." Bob scanned the shelves of their office and grabbed a jar of nails. "I'll just have to use these."

"You can't hammer those into your butt!" his brothers gasped.

"I know. I was gonna nail you two in the coal cellar."

The door opened and Boring Norman entered. He was wearing an apron that said *Kiss Me Quick, Cause I Smell* and chicken slippers, which had been a birthday present from his brothers. Norman would have liked the slippers better if they hadn't been made from his pet chooks.

"Hi guys," he said. "I've ironed your Stetsons and polished your air guns. Remember that they're not toys, so use them in a responsible and safety-conscious manner. I've only got two birds left."

"Ehmmm. One actually," Fugly replied. "I sold the other to our neighbour. He's using it to block a hole in his door, till I get round to sorting it."

"I rescued those chooks from a bag floating in the river." Norman pouted. "Someone saw three reprobates in weird hats throw it off a bridge."

"There you go using big words again," Bob scowled. "Anyone would think we let you go to school."

"Right, stepbrother." Wiggly ran a comb through his moustache, then fastened it to his face using the superglue. "We're off to the Line Dance. When we come back, we want the longhorns dry cleaned."

"And all the grazing land mowed," Wiggly added.

"Don't you think you're taking this cowboy thing a bit far?" Norman glanced out of the window where his last chicken was hopping around miserably, a pair of plastic horns attached to its head. "We don't actually have cows or a ranch. We've only got a backyard - and it's concrete."

"Yeah... well.... Just have a snack ready when we get back! Nothing fancy." Wiggly turned to his brothers. "Gophers?"

They nodded vigorously.

"Yup. Gophers. Gophers on toast."

"Ehm... This is Queensland, remember?" Norman reminded them. "There aren't any gophers in..."

"Or we could always have chicken soup."

"You want your gophers grilled or deep-fried?" Norman sighed. "I'll check at Aldi."

"Sautéed." Bob patted his cheeks. "You know I have sensitive gums."

"Can't I come to the Line Dance with you?" Norman pleaded. "I've done all the housework, hosed down your beds and even cleaned the toilet." He consulted a post-it note on the fridge. "I'll need to get more industrial solvent from the supermarket too."

"Of course not," Fugly scoffed. "Line Dancin' is for proper men."

"Seriously?"

"Of course," Bob bristled. "Men with leather chaps, tight jeans and big droopy moustaches, like the ones we just stuck on."

"You fastened it to your knee."

"I got sensitive lips, too."

"Anyway, you ain't a proper man," Fugly laughed. "You can't burp like us."

"You can't shoot like us," Wiggly added. "And you can't ride like us."

"That's because you ride in taxis and I don't get paid." Norman wouldn't give up. "I want a shot at the real thing. To win first prize on the mechanical bull!"

"Yeah?" Wiggly slapped his stepbrother on the forehead. "If you're such a great rider, how come we never see you on a horse?"

"Cause we live in the middle of Brisbane. There's nowhere to practise."

"What about Potters Park?" Fugly suggested. "It's just round the corner."

"That's a car park."

"Aw, stop nitpicking."

"I know you won't let me go because I'm just a kid." Norman looked soulfully at his stepbrothers.

"And you don't want me to get injured. But I'd be fine. Honest."

"Don't be silly, Norman. We're not letting you go because we hate you."

"If we thought you'd really get hurt," Wiggly added. "We'd chip in for your cab fare."

"How about if I go to the Line Dance and don't tell you, eh?" Norman pulled a face. "What would you do then?"

"Since you've just told us, we'd most probably shoot you."

"Oh!" Norman fastened his apron more tightly. "I suddenly remembered, I have to iron the carpet. You three have fun."

Norman was in a very bad mood. He desperately wanted to go to the Line Dance but didn't have a horse or a shooting iron. All he had was an ironing iron, which was now stuck to the carpet because Wiggly had spilt glue over the floor while applying it to his buttocks. Norman knew, if he could only enter that competition, he'd surely win the wooden Koala. He'd stay on that mechanical bull so long he'd have to take a packed lunch.

But what was the use? He had as much chance of going to the Line Dance as a porcupine has getting into a pair of tights.

Suddenly, he heard the sound of approaching hoofbeats. There was a loud crash outside and a short, masked man wearing a gold lame outfit covered in sequins burst through the door. Norman was temporarily blinded by his clothing.

"Greetings," the stranger announced. "My name ees Don Delmonte Los Trios Paranoia Delfuego el Mantovani the third. I juss move een next door."

"And you *rode* over to say hello? It's only ten yards."

"I was een a hurry. I need to borrow a letterbox, for mine seems to be meesing."

"A common occurrence round here," Norman admitted. "My brothers can probably fix it, but they'll charge you an arm and a leg."

"Ah. I had fifteen brozzer's of my own, all with deefferent mothers." The stranger gave a sigh. "We are a poor family and have donated so many body parts, there are now only twelve of us combined."

He hesitated.

"Choo look sad. Ees it because of your face?"

"It's because *my* brozzers won't let me go to the Line Dance. They say I'm too wimpy to be a cowboy."

"I can see their point." Don turned to leave and Norman's lip quivered. The brightly-clad stranger rolled his eyes.

"Ah... but what the hey! Choo can come wid *me* to the Line Dance. If choo don't mind riding bareback."

"Can't I keep my t-shirt on?" Norman asked. "I don't want to get sunburn."

"Sure. I'll put an extra saddle on my hores."

"That's not very PC."

"Hores! That choo ride. Mine ees called Dob-bin.com.au. Ees an eco-friendly alternative to Uber."

He slapped Norman on the back.

"You might even ween the wooden Koala!"

"I got no chance of weening anything," Norman sobbed. "I'm not a real cowboy. The closest I ever got to America was when my stepbrothers pushed me into the sea at Morton Bay. I don't have a hat or waistcoat or cowboy boots."

"Poor kid. I see I got here just in time." Don's accent swiftly changed. "Son. It takes more than a big water pistol to fill a ten-gallon hat, whatever that means."

He drew himself up to his full height of five foot four and thumped his chest.

"A *true* cowboy has something wonderful here."

"Nipples?"

"A pure heart, Norma."

"It's Norman. And stop calling me son." He looked Don up and down. "You can't be any older than me."

"I have a baby face." Don glanced at his youthful countenance in the mirror. "I'm actually 46 in dog years."

"Fair enough."

"Your stepbrothers?" Don waved his hand dismissively, unleashing a cloud of sequins. "They can never be true cowboys. Not if they ate so many gophers they felt like inside-out fur coats. Only real cowboys can win at a rodeo, Normal."

"My brothers won last year." Norman picked glitter out of his eye. "They beat up the other competitors."

"Really want the outfit, huh?"

"Couldn't hurt."

"Something like mine?" Don did a quick pirouette and tripped over the iron.

"Maybe a little more subtle." Norman picked him up. "You look like a heavily armed chandelier."

"OK, I'll see what I can rustle up." Don waggled his eyebrows. "Rustle! Get it?

"Ehm... Yeah." Norman regarded him suspiciously. "What's happened to your voice, by the way? Just... who are you?"

"Son. I have many names."

"I know. You strung them all together a minute ago. 'Don' is the only bit I remember."

"Fine by me." The stranger shrugged. "I may look like an exploded diamond mine but I specialise in saving damsels in distress. They love an exotic accent."

"In case you hadn't noticed, I'm a bloke."

"I know. I went to the wrong house."

"Thank God for that." Norman clasped his hands together and sank to his knees. "Please say you'll help me."

"You can help yourself, son." Don hauled him up by the hair. "All you have to do is close your peepers and sing a little song."

"A little song?"

"A magic song!"

"Oh, God."

But the stranger was his only hope, so Norman shut his eyes. Don pulled a scrap of paper from his pocket and held it up.

"Sing that."

"My eyes are closed."

"Then open one!" Don thrust the paper into his hand. "Jeez, I can't half pick em."

Norman squinted at the verse and began to croon.

Riding West across the heather.
I like guns and I like leather.
When at night my horse I tether
If he's cold, we sleep together.
Yippee aye yip, yip yippee, yip yippy.
Those rattlesnakes are long and slippy.

Norman had once taken a poetry course at Springfield town hall, though he'd actually gone to do pottery and misread the sign on the door. So, while he mused on this literary gem, Don had time to run out and buy a cowboy outfit from Mr Toy World.

"Hmmmmm.... Should be *them rattlesnakes*," Norman mused. "*Them rattlesnakes* gives the verse a more authentic western air than *those rattlesnakes*. More 'bite' if you like. Pardon the literary pun, but I do feel it fits the metaphor the poet intended."

He looked down and noticed a pile of clothes on the floor.

"Hey, what a neat trick!" He handed Don back his paper. "I don't like the metre in this either."

"Will you forget that and get your kit on!" his companion snapped. He was starting to feel sorry for the stepbrothers.

Norman did as he was told. The hat and waistcoat looked a bit small and cheap, but that's because they were made of cardboard. And the footwear was a little odd.

"These aren't cowboy boots," the boy pointed out. "They're Wellingtons."

"Son. There aint any cattle for ten miles." Don pointed out. "It *has* started raining, though."

He drew his gun and passed it over.

"Lastly, here is a pistol."

"This is yours!" Norman was genuinely touched.

"That's OK. It doesn't work." Don put both hands sternly on his hips. "Remember now. You can only keep this lovely matching hat and holster set if you uphold the first law of the cowpoke."

"Lose half my teeth and learn to play a banjo?" Norman waved the gun around maniacally.

"Nope. Be loyal, noble and true. And like poking cows."

There was a wistful look in Don's eyes, though it might have been fumes from the superglue.

"Living life in the saddle can be hard and painful, young man. Especially on your bum. My bum is always sore, Normous."

"Is it as hard and painful as washing my stepbrother's underwear?" Norman asked. "That they only take off after three months working on the building site?"

"No. Not nearly as hard and painful as that."

"I guess I'll go for it, then."

"I'm proud of you, boy. Next, you'll need a secret identity, so your brothers won't recognise you at the Line Dance." He stroked his chin. "First thing is a proper western name. Y'know, something like Billy the Kid. Got any ideas?"

"Rupert the Bear?"

"Try a handle that's a tad more masculine."

"Techno-Destructor Guy?"

"Not cowboyee enough." Don tapped his lip thoughtfully. "How about the Cinderella Kid?"

"Say, *what* now?"

"It's a bit gauche but I think it's you. And for the final part of your disguise?" He searched in his pockets. "Here we are!"

"It's a pair of glasses."

"Worked for Superman." Don plonked the spectacles on Norman's nose. "Wow! Your own parents wouldn't recognise you."

"I'm not surprised." The boy's lip quivered again. "I lost mum and dad in a boating accident."

"What happened?" Don tried hard to look like he cared.

"I went to the corner store to buy a packet of Tim Tams. When I came back, they had accidentally gone on a world cruise."

"Never mind, Normo. They live in the hearts of all righteous cowboys and in the rocks and trees besides."

"Actually, they live in Bundaberg. They just won't tell me the address."

"Whatever." Don adjusted his mask, which kept slipping down his nose. "Now follow me! Hi ho, Dobbin.com.au!"

There was a worried neighing sound from outside. Taking several ballet leaps, Don vanished out of the door.

"This guy definitely has a few stitches loose on his gun belt." Norman leaned out of the window and gave a piercing whistle.

"Taxi!"

Half an hour later, Norman was back in a state of panic, closely followed by Don.

"What are you playing at?" he railed. "You won the competition! I got so bored watching I went to get us a couple of sherbet dip-dabs. Next thing I know, you and my horse are on the Buzz bus and heading back into town."

"I saw my stepbrothers taking off in their truck. They'll have a couple of cheese daiquiris at Madam

Benbecula's House of Fluff then be back here, plastered off their faces."

"They can't hold their drink?"

"They got tiny hands like Donald Trump." Norman sighed. "Last time I didn't get my chores done before they arrived, they put Lego in my underpants and sat me on top of the spin dryer."

"Son. That's more information than I needed to know."

Norman looked down at his feet.

"Hey! I took off in such a hurry I left one of my Wellingtons stuck in the mud outside Sweaty Benny's Burger Bin."

"*What*? I borrowed these boots from Chief Break-Um-Knees All Night Camping Barn!" Don gave a groan. "He can bring down a charging buffalo using his forehead. I don't get them back, he'll be using my scrotum pole as a totem pole."

"And that's more information than *I* needed to know."

"Stay here and try not to breathe." Don ran off to retrieve the missing footwear.

Norman removed his outfit, threw it in the washing machine, grabbed a broom and started sweeping. Soon, he could hear his brothers approaching.

"Who was that masked man we passed outside?" Fugly asked. "He looked like Liberace on a horse."

"Beats me," Norman replied innocently. "How was the Line Dance?"

All three pointed their guns at him.

"Or we could chat about something else entirely."

"Let's talk about why this place isn't properly cleaned up," Wiggly snarled.

"And why supper isn't ready." Fugly peered in the oven. "There's nothing in here but three hot dogs. I bought em from the pet store yesterday and they still ain't done."

"I could only get frozen gophers," Norman explained. "They're thawing right now. How come you guys are in such a bad mood?"

"We didn't win the prize for staying on the mechanical bull." Fugly's face was black as thunder, though it was probably soot from the oven. "Some bespectacled stranger did."

"When we find him," Bob warned. "We'll show him a use for a pair of spurs he *never* considered."

"Ummmm..." Norman said nervously. "You don't happen to know who it was?"

"He looked like the Milky Bar kid with acne," Wiggly replied. "But he left before we could kill him."

"I'm so mad I could shoot my own granny." Fugly wiped his face with a half-cooked Daschund. "If I hadn't done it already."

He patted his stomach.

"I'll eat. I always eat when I'm depressed," he sighed. "What it must be doing to my waistline...

"Sure you wouldn't like a Rice Cracker instead?" Norman rummaged in the bread bin.

"No. Get those gophers now!"

Norman grabbed a handful of thawing rodents from the fridge, but they were so rigid you could have held their tails and called them hairy popsicles.

"I don't think they're quite ready."

"Right!" Bob drew his pistol. "I'm gonna plug him."

"He aint washed the dishes yet," Wiggly cautioned. "Just hit him in the arm."

"OK." Fugly squinted at Norman. "You right or left handed?"

"You mean you'd shoot your own brother?" the boy gasped.

"I don't have a problem with that."

"You don't?" Bob and Wiggly glared at him.

"Not you two!" Fugly stammered. "I mean him!"

He rounded on Norman.

"Oooooooh! Trying to cause trouble between me and my brothers, who I love almost as much as gophers on toast! I *am* gonna kill you!"

He pointed the pistol at Norman's head. The boy held the tray in front of his face, three frozen rodents still stuck to the surface. Fugly aimed at his leg instead. Norman moved the tray down.

"Stop moving that around, or I'll shoot you!"

"You're trying to shoot me anyway!" Norman tried to climb into the bin. "Try being more logical!"

There was a ring at the door. And, if there was one thing Bob hated, it was being interrupted. Before anyone could stop him… BANG! He turned and fired.

There was a thump from outside. Wiggly ran to the door and opened it.

"Yikes! You killed the mailman."

"That's OK. All we ever get is bills." Bob stared at his gun in puzzlement. "Besides, I'm a terrible shot."

"You're right." Fugly poked the body. "Looks like he electrocuted himself on the doorbell."

"I told you to get a new battery for it." Wiggly threw up his hands. "But, oh no, you thought it would be cheaper to hook the whole thing to the mains."

"I got an idea!" Bob giggled. "Let's take the body to Woollies and hide it in one of the freezers. We can lock a little kid in with it!"

"Yeah! One with claustrophobia!"

"We'll tell his mother we saw him go off in a car with two strangers."

"Those scamps," Norman grinned. "You can't help liking them."

Suddenly, there was the sound of a siren growing closer. The brothers ran around in panic, then took up martial arts stances - all being masters at Who-Flung-Dung.

"It's the law!" Fugly looked out of the window. "We gotta hide the evidence."

The stepbrothers grabbed the body and pulled it through the house. Wiggly tried to shoot Norman on the way past, but it was hard to do while dragging a dead mailman.

The brothers rushed back into the room and stood around trying to appear innocent, which was about as convincing as a drunk ostrich striving to look dainty. The door burst open and in came two policemen.

"Howdy, ya cow-tippin varmints." The leader was short and wore glasses. "I'm sheriff Cornobbler and this is my deputy Slim."

The stepbrothers gazed at him disbelievingly.

"Those uniforms look like they came from a toy store," Fugly said. "And Slim is fat."

"The correct term is big-boned," Slim sulked.

"Whatever you say," Bob shrugged. "Care for a cup of tea?"

"I ain't a drinking man, hombre." The sheriff plonked himself in an armchair. "Don't even touch water."

He grabbed a frozen gopher off the tray next to him, holding it by the tail.

"But I'll take one of these here ice lollies. I'm hotter than a skunk curry after all the chasing around I bin doing."

Norman wisely stayed silent as the sheriff took a lick and picked a few hairs off his tongue.

"I'm lookin for a boy who skedaddled from the rodeo without collectin the wooden Koala. He was in disguise but left his specs behind. I'm wearin em right now, which is why I can't actually see who I'm talking to."

He stretched his legs out and massaged them.

"I been to every bus stop, bottle shop and vegetarian restaurant in town. Me and Slim got saddle sores on our bums the size of grapefruits. Wanna see?"

"Not in the slightest," Bob muttered. "Seems a lot of trouble to go to for a wooden Koala, though."

"And $20,000 prize money."

"Oh." Bob's jaw dropped. "Well, I *was* that bespectacled man. Coincidentally."

"Actually, I think you'll find it was me," Wiggly pushed him out of the way. "I just now put my contact lenses in."

"Sheriff, the only disguises these two ever wore was when they were robbing the local K-Mart." Fugly elbowed his way forwards. "*I* am that too-modest prizewinner."

"There's one other way of finding the true identity of our mystery man." The sheriff pulled a Wellington boot from inside his trousers.

"*That* was a rather disturbing trick," Wiggly goggled. "Beats a tube of superglue any day."

"He left his wellie behind too," the lawman continued. "Whoever tries this on, an it fits, wins the prize."

The stepbrothers began yanking off their boots and Norman snapped on a surgical mask. The air was filled with a smell like a month-old prawn cocktail in an Egyptian boiler room.

"I gotta admit." The sheriff held his nose. "That tootsie odour is certainly excessive."

"S'cuse me." Slim put a hand over his mouth and ran for the bathroom.

The brothers tugged and pulled but none of them could get the boot to fit.

"Maybe if I took my socks off as well," Bob suggested.

"I believe that's against the Geneva Convention." The lawman yanked the Wellington back. "Looks like you sheep-shimmyin grease weasels is outta luck."

"Hey!" Norman broke in. "What about me?"

"You!" The brothers chuckled. "Don't make us laugh. Oh, too late."

"I *am* supposed to try everyone," the sheriff shrugged. "Even this obvious loser."

He threw the boot to Norman while his stepbrothers hooted and jeered. None of them noticed he had been wearing one identical Wellington the whole time.

Norman pulled it on.

"See? A perfect fit."

"Well… stick a rattler in my pasta and call it a noisy noodle." The sheriff scratched his head. "You win, son."

"I'll have my money in traveller's cheques, please!" Norman did a little dance. "You can post my pyjamas to the Bahamas!"

"Now I'm REALLY gonna kill him." Bob pulled out his gun.

"This boy is now under my protection, lads." The lawman stepped forwards. "The fact that I'd like to step on him then scrape him back off don't change anything."

"Insult me all you like," Norman grinned. "I'm rich."

"All right, pea brain," the sheriff shrugged. "Ready to go, Slim?"

"Absolutely." His companion appeared back in the room. "I tried to throw up in the toilet, but a dead mailman in the bath put me off."

"Oh, my." The sheriff folded his arms. "Unless it's a family heirloom, I'm gonna have to run y'all in."

"Yeah?" Wiggly leapt to his feet. "Eat lead, gopher licker!"

The stepbrothers went for their guns, and the air was filled with flying lead. When the smoke had cleared, Norman, Slim and the sheriff were completely unhurt.

"Told you I was a rotten shot," Bob groaned.

"Jeez." The sheriff patted himself. "When hunting season rolls around, entire forests must flock to *your* backyard."

The brothers dropped their weapons and ran out of the door. There was a loud crash outside and a surprised whinnying sound.

"Aren't you going to go after them?" Norman turned to the sheriff.

"I think you'll find they're embedded in my horse."

He removed his glasses and Norman gave a gulp.
"*Don*?"

"Told you they worked as a disguise." Don jerked a thumb at Slim. "My name is actually Harlan McFarlan, boy detective. This is my associate, Fats."

"I don't mind being called Slim, though," Fats blushed. "I think it suits me."

"Thanks for saving me, guys." Norman shook their hands warmly. "I guess I'll just take my $20,000 and be off."

"I'm shocked, Nomad!" Harlan's face fell. "I thought you wanted to be a cowboy? A cowboy's life is supposed to be one of self-sacrifice and pain, not flaunting your large assets in front of dusky Mexican beach attendants. You have a hard and windy path to take."

"I'd rather just take the money."

"Buddy." Fats massaged his large butt. "That money should go to the Bellbowrie Institute for Research into the Treatment of Incurable Anal Sores. After a few years on a horse, you'll be glad you used it for that end."

"Nice use of the double entendre there, partner," Harlan nodded.

"You're right!" Norman slapped his knee. "I don't need the money! From now on, it's the open range for me, with the steer as my friend and a cow pat as my pillow.

"That's the spirit."

"Goodbye, masked man. I don't suppose I'll ever remember your name." Norman gave Harlan a cowboy salute and disappeared into the sunset.

"Sure you will." Harlan pocketed the $20,000. "It's gonna be on plenty of wanted posters come morning."

"That's a bit mean." Fats raised an eyebrow. "He won the prize fair and square. Leave him half the money."

"*What*?"

"Do the right thing, buddy."

"How do you know he'll even come back?" Harlan complained.

"It's raining and he's only wearing underpants."

"You're too nice, Fats, know that?"

"Call me Slim again. I really like Slim."

"How about a compromise," Harlan grinned. "Fat Boy Slim?"

"How about I give you a kick in the testicles?"

"I take back what I said about you being nice." Harlan counted out half the cash and stuck it on top of the oven. "Never mind. There are plenty more suckers out there to con."

Fats glared at him.

"I mean, plenty more innocent victims who need our detecting help."

"That's better."

And off they went, singing their cowboy song.

Bunny Wunny Woo

A few years ago, I took part in an anti-war march on Princes Street. Or maybe it was pro-war. I was nipping out of the office for a cheese roll, so I was only in it for five minutes.

Being lunchtime, most of the sandwich makers were on their break and they'd taken up the entire window watching the parade. A police horse had done a huge shit in the road and they were taking bets on who would stand in it first. My money was on the guy with stilts, dressed as Death.

Suddenly, there was a huge cheer behind me. A toddler had sat down in the mess, scooped up a handful and threw it at his mum. The workers in the sandwich shop went wild, waving and filming the incident to post on YouTube.

That's when I decided to become an entertainer.

I quit my job in sales and enrolled in Dunfermline College of Drama. It used to be a polytechnic, teaching joiners and the like. I think they must have kept some of the old lecturers, too. I was taught wooden acting and spent a lot of time pretending to be a tree.

My gamble paid off, however. I got an agent within seven years of graduating and, a few months after that, moved into TV roles. I was 'woman in fish van' in *Monarch of the Glen* and 'pedestrian who falls over' in *River City*, though you can only see my feet waving in the air. Eventually, I got typecast as 'dead body in bath' in a dozen crime series, on account of my natural resistance to wrinkling and ability to lie motionless in cold water for long periods of time.

Then, just as I was sure my big break was around the corner, I got pregnant. I'd dreamed of marrying a childhood sweetheart but I didn't have one, so I ended up with a childhood acquaintance instead.

When little Bryant was born, I took him to one of my acting jobs - playing 'body found in dumpster' in an episode of *Taggart*. The director spotted Bryant and cast him as 'plain baby in pram'. He appeared in four scenes and got a bigger cheque than me, even though he wasn't a member of *Equity*.

That kind of success eluded my husband, a struggling playwright specialising in horror. He tended to cast me in his shows, so it was handy I had so much experience playing dead. Even so, it's hard to lie on the floor of an Edinburgh Fringe performance, staring sightlessly at an audience of seven, who look more lifeless than you.

We didn't give up, though. The glass is either half empty or half full. In the end, we emptied and filled it quite a bit, which probably didn't help our careers.

In the last few months, however, my husband appeared to be making a real effort to pull himself together. He seemed more self-assured. His thinning hair had developed white flecks, prominent at the temples, so he had it cut short. Didn't grow a goatee for compensation. He looked pretty good. Better than when I met him. I wondered if he had found someone else.

One night, as we drank wine, he said.

"Sometimes, I feel like a character in one of my own stories. I can make myself do this or that but it's like I'm describing my feelings rather than experiencing them." He drained his glass. "Maybe I should stop writing and start living. Try getting a proper job."

I nodded, not daring to jump on the idea while my husband was still deciding if it was safe to climb up. Also, I couldn't tell if he was serious or thinking up lines for a new play.

The next week, he came home with Bunny Wunny Woo.

"And what exactly is that?"

It was upside down on one of the pine kitchen chairs. Its head hung down over the seat, black candy-floss hair dusting the floor. The arms dangled in mock surrender, or perhaps a gravity-defying handstand, bent awkwardly at elbow and wrist. Its head was too big for the malnourished wooden body and the jaw was twisted and splintered, as if some almighty haymaker had propelled it over the back of the chair and into its present position. Now it lay unconscious, stunned or dead. Its eyes should have been closed, crossed or sightlessly staring so I could tell which.

But it didn't have eyes, only empty sockets.

"That," said my husband. "Is Bunny Wunny Woo."

"Is it now?" I replied.

My husband hasn't really paid the attention to our son that I'd like. Not the sort, I suppose. He never had a pet in his life and, as far as I know, doesn't remember to water plants. He sometimes joked about his reluctance to hold Bryant.

"There's nothing to the little man yet. Doesn't seem quite real."

He didn't say it like he expected this attitude to change.

He'd brought home toys for Bryant before, though I often wondered if that was just a way of keeping him quiet. Bunny Wunny Woo was different. The broken body would take a lot of work and its face needed re-painted.

But Bunny Wunny Woo wasn't *for* Bryant.

"I've got a great idea for a horror play," my husband said.

"I take it the dummy will feature heavily."

"Absolutely!" He held up Bunny Wunny Woo. "Ventriloquist dolls are innately creepy."

This one was. There was nothing innate about it. My husband seemed pleased by that.

"Where did you get it?" I asked.

"Found him in a bin," said my husband. "I'm going to fix him. I'll learn how to do the voice."

"Ventriloquism?"

"Why not?"

"It looks like someone beat him up."

"I'll speak for him. I'll sort him."

"Where'd he get that stupid name?"

My husband pulled back the dummy's collar, revealing a scrawny unpainted wooden neck.

"It's written on a tag."

He wiggled Bunny Wunny Woo's head at me. The broken jaw bounced slackly, held only by a couple of loose gut tendons. My husband spoke out of the side of his mouth.

How do you do?
I'm Bunny Wunny Woo
My eyes are broken
My jaw is too
But I'll get fixed and be good as new

"Very impressive, honey."

My husband began writing his horror play and seemed remarkably sure it would be a big success. He hired a room with a stage in Wilkie House, down in the Cowgate. Got some flyers made up advertising the show. I argued that Bunny Wunny Woo wasn't a very creepy name, but my husband was adamant.

"It'll get people wondering," he winked.

"About your sanity?"

To be honest, the plot was pretty standard stuff about a ventriloquist dummy that slowly takes over a family. I played the disgruntled mother who, of course, ends up dying. My husband played the husband who doesn't notice anything is wrong.

Nothing like a bit of typecasting.

My husband began to fix up Bunny Wunny Woo. He got a set of false teeth, cut a bit to size, and painted the face. I watched him shape and paint and attach, half impressed, half bored. And with an indefinable fraction of unease. He had bought a large gooey rubber eye from the joke shop. It was a bounce ball, one of those things you throw at the wall and it sticks. He cut it in half and glued them into the empty sockets.

"There we go."

The eyeballs stared. My husband put his hand inside Bunny Wunny Woo's jacket. The jaw clicked open and shut like a little piranha, eyes wide and emotionless to match.

"It looked creepy before. Now it would give Charley Manson nightmares."

How do you do?
I'm Bunny Wunny Woo
My eyes are starey
My jaw is scary
But I'm not as hairy as my Auntie Mary

The jaw moved pretty well. My husband's lips moved too, rather obviously. He looked at Bunny Wunny Woo's blank face and I looked at his.

"What? I'm still working on it."

I admit, the lines of his new play were better than usual. Easy to learn, even if there were a lot of them. By two days before the show, I had them three-quarters down. All good actresses do it that way.

"You remember I agreed to look after William tomorrow afternoon?" I asked. "While I'm going over my lines."

William is my sister's boy. He's a quiet little thing and, if I'm honest, he's a bit slow. I hadn't seen him since Bryant was born but I figured looking after him was a good rehearsal for when my own son got older. I suppose you could call it life imitating art.

"Tell him not to mess with Bunny Wunny Woo," my husband warned.

"I doubt he'd touch it if I gave him a barge pole."

"Claire, he's just a little dummy," my husband huffed. "What harm can he be to anyone?"

William arrived next afternoon. My lines weren't *quite* learned yet. Bunny Wunny Woo wasn't entirely fixed. My husband had gone for a walk because the house wasn't big enough to contain his pacing.

William was no trouble to look after, though. I knew he liked being creative - it must run in the family - so I'd bought some crayons and a pad for him at the Spar. When he arrived, Bunny Wunny Woo was sitting at the dining table, legs sticking straight out. William gave a little start.

Bunny Wunny Woo had splints fastened to his broken arms. My husband had applied glue to the snapped limbs and the wood kept everything in place while it dried. He looked like he was strapped in an electric chair, sitting like that. I put a large tartan blanket on the floor for William to kneel on.

"Here's a colouring book," I smiled. "Aunt Claire's got some work to do, so she's going to the kitchen."

I went next door and got my script out. Did a few vocal exercises and resisted the temptation to practise being dead. I couldn't work with Bunny Wunny Woo until his glue dried, so I put a sock over my hand instead.

Stand in for ventriloquist dummy. I knew how the sock felt.

I felt a tug at my leg. It was William.

"The big doll lookin at me." His eyes were tearful.

"The big doll can't harm you, honey."

"I don' like it. Scary, lookin at me."

"His name's Bunny Wunny Woo."

"Bun oh oh. Oh."

"That's right. Aunt Claire's a bit occupied, ok?"

"S'awright."

He turned and waddled off back to the dining room.

How do you do?
I'm Bunny Wunny Woo
With eyes to see
And a jaw to chew
Now we've gotten in a stew
You fixed me and I'll fix you

There was another tug at my leg.

"Big doll talking to me. Scare me."

"William. Aunt Claire is very busy."

"Take big doll away."

"What's the doll saying?"

"Don' know."

"Aunt Claire can't move Bunny Wunny Woo until his glue dries. But he's not going to harm you and I really have to work."

"S'ugly. Scary." William looked tearful again.

"Tell you what," I said brightly. "Why don't you take your blanket and put it over Bunny Wunny Woo! Then you can't see him and he can't see you."

"Ok." William padded back into the dining room.

I made myself a cup of tea and started back on the lines, grateful for silence at last.

C'mon, he's just a little dummy. What harm can he be to anyone?

The script dropped from my hand and I ran to the dining room, skidding on the polished kitchen floor. Bunny Wunny Woo was sitting on my husband's chair, mouth open, staring with its dead fish eyes. William was on the floor scribbling furiously.

Bryant's crib was in the corner, his motionless body covered by a large tartan blanket.

William didn't look up.

"Ugly doll can't see me anymore," he said.

Shaggy Dog

The Muir twins had just turned 35 years old and, as a birthday celebration, built a bomb. Pretty good one too. It had a little clock attached, with wires and two Smartie tubes wrapped in duct tape that could have contained any amount of Gelignite or whatever, but actually still contained Smarties.

Once completed, the would be terrorists put their fake bomb in a plastic Safeways carrier bag and carted it up to Kirriemuir town square. They found young Div hanging around outside Vissocchi's and bribed him with a couple of cigarettes to deliver it to Mike's Mealstore as a practical joke. Mike's Mealstore was a little shop tucked behind the turret of the chemist store at the top of Bellie's Brae. For an entire pack of Benson and Hedges, Div would probably have delivered it naked to the Houses of Parliament.

Young Div sauntered into the meal store, whistling loudly. He dropped the Safeways bag casually onto the floor and, with a deft backheel, scooted it between two bins of mixed nuts, rather a cavalier treatment for an unexploded device. This entire pantomime was noted with suspicion by Mike himself, who had been watching young Div like a hawk the moment he set foot on the premises. For any teenager to enter the shop and sneakily try to leave something, rather than remove it, was quite a novelty. In fact, to have a teenager come in at all was somewhat of an event, since dried bran wasn't high on their list of shopliftable items. Especially with a pharmacy next door.

After Div had gone, Mike retrieved the bag and opened it.

"Some folk must think I came up the Tay on a banana boat," he snorted.

Seconds later, the Muir twins saw their precious bomb fly out the back door and land in an alley.

None of this concerned me. I had a party to go to. Oss was throwing a big bash out at Erroll and, by the looks of things, this shindig would make the Nuremberg Rally look like a cart race.

According to my mate, Ed, there was a huge barn next to the bothy, perfect for a good old boogie, with drugs and booze galore. Oss had hired a mobile disco and everything. Cars were setting off days early just to be sure of finding the place... where the hell was Erroll, anyway? Somewhere near Perth was all we knew. Even Pod was on his way down from Loch Snechie with a van full of co-workers from the Hydro-electric plant. If a fuse blew up at Snechie in the next few days, the whole east coast of Scotland would be in darkness till they got back.

On Saturday afternoon, our own little convoy set off. In the lead was Ed astride his Honda, then Big Norma, Big Ethel and Paul in Big Norma's Mini. Next came Bob and Doug in Doug's Vauxhall, Miracle 1, so-called because it took a miracle to get it started.

"It's a collector's item," Doug told us proudly. "The bin men have tried to collect it three times already."

Bringing up the rear were me and Hilly on Hilly's green Kawasaki. Hilly didn't like to be at the back but it was difficult to pass the Vauxhall and Mini, who were driving side by side so Doug and Big Norma could have an argument. Hilly was further hampered by the sixteen cans of lager in a rucksack I had slung over my shoulder which, every time we went around a corner, caused enough centrifugal force to tip over a buffalo. Since the Kawasaki now required the same manoeuvring time and space as a Canard liner, Hilly was forced to slow down for inconveniences - like hairpin bends, junctions and crossing pedestrians - a concept he didn't normally entertain.

We solved the problem by riding up the grass verge by the road and launching the rucksack through Doug's open rear window. The Vauxhall was already carrying more alcohol than the average pub chain and the added weight meant Doug could only make the turnoff for the bothy by slowing down somewhere around Forfar, a process further complicated by the fact that the signpost for Erroll was hidden by an entire forest - a common trick in Perthshire for deterring unwanted tourism. Since Doug was also carrying Ed's booze, the Honda stuck doggedly to the Vauxhall's tail, as did Big Norma, who thought it was a game.

"It's like bloody Wacky Races on Acid," Hilly grunted sourly. He whirled into the hidden turnoff at an angle worthy of any Greek mathematician, then rocketed up the wood-lined dirt track towards the bothy. The rest of our motley convoy disappeared down the main road and round the thickly wooded hills until they eventually found themselves on the other side of Oss's property.

Doug didn't fancy taking his car across the rutted fields to the makeshift car park, in case all he was left with was the steering wheel. So he, Bob, Ethel, Ed, Norma and Paul divided up the alcohol and carried it across the fields to the barn - a feat of manpower that would put most pyramid builders to shame.

Hilly stopped halfway up the hill.

"Got to go in with a bit of class, eh?"

He pulled two cans of Superlager from inside his biker jacket and opened them.

"Here. Hold these."

He gunned the engine and we roared off again. I tried to drink one of the cans straight away, so I'd have a hand free to hold onto the bike, but the G-forces raised by Hilly's rate of acceleration wouldn't allow the beer anywhere near my face.

The Honda crested the hill with all the grace of pro-jectile phlegm in a high wind. Floating past on the right was the barn, already pulsing with music, lights and hormones. To the left, two babes were perched on a low wall, having a smoke in the fading light. In the middle of the track was a line of rocks that Oss had planted as a homemade speed bump-come-joke.

The bike hit one of the rocks at just over the speed of sound, so it wasn't even worth screaming as we shot into the air. Defying the law of gravity, which was Hilly's speciality anyway, both he and the bike re-turned to earth far more rapidly than I did. In fact, I'd done a complete somersault before I realised I'd lost contact with the machine entirely.

Next thing I knew, I was flat on my back on a patch of grass below the two smoking girls, having miracu-lously missed them, the wall they were sitting on, a sea of gutters, several half bricks, and a couple of gorse bushes. I could see right up their miniskirts, admiring a couple of pairs of sturdy thighs in black woollen tights. I held a can of foaming lager up to each girl.

"Fancy a drink, ladies?"

They giggled and accepted. That was our dates sorted for the night.

Hilly, still attached to the Honda by some fluke of science, rode back over.

"Nice one, bud," he grinned, "Didnae spill a drop."

Meanwhile, Pod had run into some difficulty on the journey south. Just outside Froikham, a train track intersected the road. As his van approached the crossing, lights began to flash, signalling the arrival of a train, and a red and white striped barrier descended to cut off road traffic.

Pod, under the influence of too many *Smokey and the Bandit* movies or, perhaps just under the influence, slammed his foot on the accelerator. The van narrowly made it, scraping under the barrier and rattling into Froikham at a velocity that threatened to pull grazing farm animals into its slipstream. Fortunately, this child-killing speed was cut short by contact with a large Rottweiler sitting placidly in the middle of the main road. The van hit the dog a glancing blow and came to an immediate halt, but the Rottweiler was catapulted in a perfect arc, landing head-first in a bin. Pod couldn't have aimed better if he'd been the world basketdog champion.

"A perfect example of opposite and equal forces at work," one of the Hydro-electric workers noted, Hydro-electric workers knowing about that kind of thing. Judging by the look of surprise as it flew through the air, however, this had been the dog's first encounter with Newtonian principles.

Pod, demonstrating mettle that made great physicists like Oppenheimer invent the atomic bomb, stuck the van into gear and drove off down the nearest side street before anyone spotted him. As a result of this rerouting, he missed the turnoff for Erroll and ended up on the wrong side of Oss's bothy, where he parked next to Doug and Norma's cars.

This may seem an insignificant detail in itself, but it's important for the story later on.

The party in the barn must have been a huge success for, next day, nobody could remember a thing about it. I woke up on the bothy's bedroom floor with one of the teenage girls snoring loudly beside me, but my attempts to roll her into another room only succeeded in waking her up. I vaguely recalled her name might be Mary but decided not to chance my luck by calling her anything.

We slouched into the living room. Oss was lying on the couch in a stupor and Bob was in the middle of the floor rolling a breakfast joint. Two or three strangers sat in a grey haze, smoking John Player Special and eating toast. Doug and Ed were standing, staring blearily out the window, trying to figure out where they were. The whole room had the stale, musty morning smell of waking bodies, cigarettes, dope and coffee.

I joined them at the window, shielding my gaze from the dazzling glare outside. Ed didn't have to. His eyes weren't open yet. It had begun snowing about ten o clock the evening before and continued heavily all night. Now, in the weak morning sun, the land around the bothy was an unbroken sea of white. Parked cars slumbered like rusty foam-flecked rocks and myriad tents dotted the fields around the barn, like sailboats anchored off some crumbling wooden island.

"Isn't that beautiful?" I enthused, properly moved by nature's glory.

"Fuck off." Ed had managed to get one eye open and it looked like a half-sucked gobstopper. He stumbled back to a chair and I returned to my date to see if she had a name tag sticking out somewhere. Doug remained at the window, more from inertia than any enjoyment of the view. Eventually, he spoke.

"There's a police car coming up the drive."

Eyebrows were raised all round. Only Oss seemed nonplussed.

"They'll just be here to check we didnae burn the place to the ground last night," he yawned from the depths of the couch. "We didn't burn the place to the ground last night, did we?"

Doug assured him that we hadn't.

"Och, I'll away an talk to them, then." Oss struggled to his feet and pulled on a pair of worn slippers shaped like rabbits. "Just dinnae wave that joint around near the window."

He went outside and trudged towards the parked panda car. The bunny ears flapped up and down on the snow leaving faint imprints. Doug kept up a running commentary on his progress.

"Oss is talking to the polis now and they look like they're having some kind of argument. Oss is waving his arms about. Hmmmmm. There's another police car coming up the drive now and..... eh.... another one."

Joints were quickly stubbed out, blocks of Red-Leb and packets of hash vanishing into shoes, plant pots and leftover snacks. A note of consternation had crept into Doug's voice.

"Oss is fighting with a couple of the polis. He's just booted one in the knacks. Nice one, Oss! Now they've got him on the ground. Oh. That looks painful."

Loyalty to our host brought the occupants of the room reluctantly to their feet. Obstruction of justice was a pretty serious thing, but we couldn't just let the police beat Oss up without at least going outside to watch. We headed for the front door.

"Now there's an army truck coming up the hill."

We trooped back into the living room again.

"An army truck?"

"Yeah. And it's full of soldiers." Doug sounded genuinely surprised, as if he expected an army truck to be full of chartered accountants.

We clustered round the window.

"Fuck me," said Ed with equally misplaced disbelief. "They've got guns. And there's another truck coming up behind."

The entire invasion was the fault of the Muir twins. They'd been left with a useless fake bomb that wouldn't have fooled a one-eyed granny. But it had taken them a whole afternoon to build and they were bloody well determined to get a rise out of someone. Eventually, they had a flash of inspiration and left it under a police car in the middle of Kirriemuir town square before leaving for Errol.

The fact that the Muir twins had been able to crawl under a panda car and leave their suspicious package in full view of the police station, without any cops spotting them, didn't bode well for the prevention of an actual terrorist attack - especially since the driver was sitting inside the vehicle at the time. However, getting out to buy a Curly-Wurly, he caught his foot in the seat belt and landed flat on his face, giving him a perfect view of the device lodged behind his front wheel.

Within an hour, the entire town square had been cordoned off and a bomb disposal unit was on its way.

Four hours later, the army sergeant and the police sergeant sat on the station bench in furious silence. On the other side of the car park, police and squaddies were playing five-a-side with the remains of the device. The police were losing.

"You have no idea," growled the police sergeant, "What I would give to know what bastards did this." The army sergeant grunted his agreement.

Young Div's head appeared round the side of the police station wall, an extremely unusual place for Div's head to be.

"Hey there, loons," he chirped. "You wouldnae happen tae have cigarettes on you, by any chance?"

We stared, open-mouthed, as two giant green mud-splattered lorries thundered into the yard outside the bothy, and armed soldiers poured from the rear. On hitting the frozen ground, most of them landed flat on their backs with their legs sticking up, while the rest pinwheeled madly, loosing off random shots as they fought to keep their balance. A dozen tent flaps flew open and startled sleepy heads appeared, their torpor turning to astonishment, then horror, as they took in the scene. A few perceptive campers, realising that there were more drugs and potentially underage girls in their tents than most Arabian slave caravans, threw on coats and darted half-naked for their cars. Leading the pack were the Muir twins, who had immediately figured out what the army was doing there.

The soldiers no longer cared to single out one particular target. The sight of fleeing panic-stricken civilians had aroused in them an atavistic military response and they were ready to rape and pillage anything that wasn't nailed down. One armed section moved to cut off access to the parked cars, a classic military manoeuvre hampered only by a flock of ducks attacking their legs. The rest of the soldiers fixed bayonets and attacked, followed at a safe distance by truncheon-waving police. Several burly squaddies broke off from the main push and headed straight for the bothy.

"Shit," Doug said. "This place doesn't have a back door."

Ed was already in the rear bathroom, trying desperately to prize open a window.

"It's painted shut!" he yelled. "What does Oss do for ventilation, stick a straw through a fucking crack in the wall?"

We rushed to join him and our luck was in. There, above the toilet, was a small grimy aperture, open just a crack... if you'll excuse the pun. Me, Doug, Bob, Mary, Ed and Big Norma squeezed into the tiny loo, which must have been some sort of unsanitary record and Doug climbed onto the cistern to open the window further. We heard several loud crashes as troopers leapt through the front windows of the bothy, rather unnecessary, since the door was open. There, they commenced battle with the rest of the occupants, who had unwisely decided to turn Oss's living room into their main defensive position.

"Lock the bog door," urged Ed. "It'll buy us some time."

Bob looked down.

"It doesn't have a lock," he said. "It doesn't even have a handle."

Doug was already worming his lanky body through the bathroom window.

"It's a pretty big drop out here," he called back. "Slippy too. I don't think I can really... Wooooah!!!!"

Then he was gone.

"Whatever happened to ladies first?" Big Norma scowled.

"We're not on the fucking Titanic, you know." Bob snapped.

"Ach, I'm not a lady anyway," Norma remembered. "And I'll never fit through that wee gap."

Ed and I gazed at her enormous breasts, something we frequently did, nodding in agreement. Big Norma barrelled back out into the living room.

"She's gonna take on the army herself," I said admiringly. "Brave lass. Hope they brought an anti-tank gun."

"Aw, shit." Ed was trying to heave himself on the cistern. "I've stood in the sodding toilet."

"Hasn't been flushed either," I pointed out.

"Dirty bastards!"

Bob helpfully pulled the handle.

"Thanks a lot." Ed lifted his leg and looked at the stain spreading up to his knee. There was a splintering sound from next door and he toppled back into the toilet again.

"Someone just threw a crash helmet through the bedroom window." Doug's voice floated in from outside. Big Norma had obviously found an alternative means of escape.

"Great," muttered Ed, launching himself through the bathroom window. "I was needing that in case some tosser decides to shoot me in the head."

As if on cue, there was a burst of rifle fire from the living room and the rest of us made a mad dash for freedom. Bob and I made it through the gap, along with a shower curtain and half a Venetian blind, landing in a heap in the snow. We turned and saw Mary's hands scrabbling at the opening as she tried vainly to pull herself out.

We grabbed an arm each and heaved till her head, then her torso, squeezed through the window. A look of horror crossed her face as she realised her bum was too big to fit into the gap. Moved by chivalric impulse, Bob and I put one foot each on the bothy wall, then tugged with all our might.

"Dinnae!" Mary squealed. "You're pulling ma fucking hips off."

"Go back," I advised, pushing at her face. "The bedroom window's bigger."

"Are you saying I need to go on a diet?"

"Just get back in!"

"I cannae! My feet won't reach the toilet!"

Bob and I looked at each other. The rest of our fugitive band were cowering in a ditch behind us, making furious beckoning and slitting throat motions. Mary gazed at me with pleading eyes as another burst of rifle fire rattled the house. It was all very romantic and World War II.

"Stay alive," I said. "Wherever you are, wherever they take you, I'll find you. I promise. I will... find you."

"Get me out of here, you wanker."

Bob and I shrugged, then jumped into the ditch.

By now, the army had crushed all resistance and taken control of the bothy - but they didn't want to pursue us through the jagged bedroom window in case it snagged their uniforms - and Mary's bum had effectively sealed the bathroom exit. It gave us the precious seconds we needed.

"I'll never forget her," I sighed as we crawled along the bottom of the ditch. "I wish I'd gotten her phone number... or her proper name, at least."

"That lassie's arse saved our lives," Bob agreed.

We scooted through the frost on our hands and knees, following Doug, Ed and Big Norma. The ditch was free of water but, even so, our extremities were soon completely numb which, in Big Norma's case, took a bit of doing. Though the rest of the battling partygoers were cut off from their vehicles, the ravine we had landed in ran across the fields in the opposite direction, passing close to the isolated spot where Doug and Big Norma had parked.

Panting and blubbering with cold and exertion, we crawled through the freezing snow, heads down, puffs of crystalline breath shooting from our gasping mouths, aware only speed could save us from getting frozen, shot, imprisoned or, at least, suffering a severe kicking.

After a hundred yards, I figured it was safe enough to risk a peek at what was going on back at the bothy and gingerly raised my head over the rim.

It was a truly incredible sight. People were running in all directions across snow-draped, picture-postcard fields, chased by armed assailants. Most of the fugitives were half-dressed, some were completely naked and those who had already been apprehended were being herded, shivering, into a disused pig-pen, surrounded by bayonet wielding guards. Some of the more intrepid defenders had climbed onto the barn roof and were holding off their attackers with pitchforks. The scene looked like Dante's Inferno at Christmas.

We got as close to the parked cars as possible without leaving our shelter. Cautiously, we slid out of the protective furrow and wriggled across the frozen ground towards safety. The pitched battle was now half a mile away and we slowly narrowed the gap to safety, grinning through chattering teeth, unaware that several pairs of eyes were focused on us from the dark interior of the only other vehicle in the vicinity.

Pod's van.

Pod and the Hydro-electric workers had been up to date on the impending weather, Hydro-electric workers knowing about that sort of thing. So they opted to spend the night in their transportation rather than alfresco. Woken by the sound of gunfire in the morning, they had spent an entertaining half-hour brewing coffee on a portable stove and watching the altercation.

Now their neutrality was threatened by a half dozen frost coated figures crawling out of a ditch towards them.

"Look out, lads," Pod cried. "Stormtroopers on a sneaky attack."

"Storm ditch troopers," one of the Hydro-electric workers corrected, but Pod was already in the driver's seat. With a throaty early morning growl, his van roared to life, huge clouds of steam pouring from its exhaust, as he backed warily away.

Ed leapt to his feet, waving both arms.

"Pod! It's us. Wait! It's your friends, you stupid fucking moron!"

His wispy blonde hair was frosted in an arc round his head and he bobbed up and down like a Crested Grebe.

Too late. Pod's van thundered off down the hill. As the sound of its engine faded into the distance, we became aware of an ominous silence behind us.

Slowly, we turned.

The melee at the bothy had completely stopped, each participant frozen in mid-thwack, every one staring up the hill at us.

"Oops."

Leaping to our feet, we sprinted for the cars, slipping and sliding and covering the distance in a manner that would have surely won us a place in the Winter Olympics, irrespective of the event. Halfway to his bike, Ed toppled over.

"My leg's frozen!" he screamed, looking in dismay at one toilet-coated, frosted limb, sticking straight in the air. With a sob, he began dragging himself hand over hand towards us like some mutant stick insect.

Back at the bothy, several rozzers were making a dash for their police cars and one army truck stuttered into life. Doug was now fumbling madly at the door of his car.

"My bloody fingers have gone all numb. Norma, let me put my hands up your sweater."

Norma already had her engine running. With a sigh, she got back out of the Mini, strode over to Doug's car and gave a mighty tug on the door handle. It came off.

"That's what happens when you drive a pile of shite." Norma climbed back into her car and sped off.

"Never mind, Doug," Bob opened the passenger door. "I forgot to lock this side."

Soon, we were also zig-zagging down the hill towards the B-road that wound away from Erroll. From the rear window, we could see Ed had managed to reach the Honda and pull himself onto it, but he lacked enough motor response in his foot to kick start it. Eventually, it overturned on top of him.

Then we were on the road proper and heading for Kirriemuir, scattering wildlife and sailing past Big Norma, who had stopped briefly to empty a pile of joint ends out of her ashtray. Doug stuck *Black and White* by the Stranglers into his old car stereo and turned up the volume to a point where the vibrations dislodged snow from passing trees.

"Excellent getaway music, lads," he enthused.

There was a loud parping behind us and Big Norma drew up alongside.

"Better get your skates on," she mouthed, jerking her thumb behind. Looking in the rear mirror, we could see an army truck and a police car following at top speed.

"Shit!" Doug slammed his foot on the accelerator and the speedometer moved forward about half a millimetre.

"Do you think the police got our licence number?" I peered anxiously behind, trying to gauge the distance between them and us.

"I doubt it," Doug said confidently. "The plates fell off last week."

"Can we outrun them?"

"How would I know? We're in a car."

That's when we hit the patch of ice.

Every good driver knows the last thing to do when you hit ice is to brake. Doug slammed on the footbrake, pulled on the handbrake and would have thrown an anchor out the window, if we'd been carrying one. Fortunately, the Vauxhall's balding tyres had such a tenuous relationship with the surface of the road they didn't notice the difference. Doug whisked over the ice as if it had never been there. Big Norma's regularly serviced wheels, however, registered the change in surface tension immediately and the Mini went into a Kamikaze spin. Being an excellent driver, Big Norma kept her foot firmly on the accelerator with the result that, several revolutions later, her car catapulted down the road at twice the velocity it had being going before.

Big Norma roared approval and banged her head triumphantly against the steering wheel before realising that she was heading back in the direction she'd come. Rattling towards her, filling the entire road, was the army truck.

Norma jerked the steering wheel to the left, the army driver jerked his to the right and both vehicles missed each other by inches, careening into the surrounding forest. Norma managed to bring the Mini under control by running into a tree, counting on the buffering quality of her breasts to avoid serious concussion. The army driver tried to apply the same slowing down process and demolished several Scots Pines, before picking something larger and steering his truck into the side of a cottage.

Doug kept the pedal to the metal but we knew there was still a police car somewhere behind, that could easily overtake us before we got to safety. Come to think of it, in Doug's car, old age could overtake us before we got to safety.

"We need to get to find a bit of civilisation so we can blend in," said Doug. "Froikham's up ahead."

"Fine," I smiled. "If it's morning rush hour, there'll be at least three cars on the main road. We can blend in with them."

"Look at that," Bob gawped as Froikham suddenly hove into view.

'That' was the rear of Pod's van, sticking into the air like a rusty thumb. The front end was wedged securely in a roadside ditch and two banana-shaped tyre tracks in the snow left ample evidence of the point where Pod had skidded off the road. Pod and the Hydro-electric workers were sitting glumly by the wreck, trying to hitch a lift.

"What a sound guy," said Bob. "He swerved rather than hit that dog."

Sitting placidly in the middle of the street was a large Rottweiler with a bandage around its head.

"Interesting place, Froikham." Doug waved one digit cheerfully at Pod as he roared past. "Bit weird, though."

Bob frowned.

"Up ahead. Look. The train barrier's down."

"There must be a train coming," Doug said.

"Naw. They let it stay down on Sunday to give it a rest."

"Lads. The police car's gonna be here any minute."

"Shit." Bob looked round in panic. "Drive through the barrier before the train gets here."

"I don't know." Doug stroked his chin doubtfully. "It's at least an inch thick. Plywood, too."

"Then, let's double back."

But it was too late. We could hear a police siren growing louder behind us.

"Try to look inconspicuous." Doug grabbed a grimy rag from under the dashboard. "Pretend we live here and we're washing the car."

"Doug. It's snowing."

Our pursuers rounded the corner and slid to a halt a few feet away. The doors flew open and four burly policemen emerged, grinning triumphantly. They unfastened their truncheons and advanced.

"Jesus." Bob gasped. "Their foreheads are wider than their chests."

To make matters worse, the train finally turned up, thundering over the crossing with a deafening roar and drowning out the sound of us pleading for our lives.

"Lock the door!" cried Doug. "Oh shit. Mine doesn't have a handle. We're dead."

"I don't know about that," I said. "Look out the back window."

Perhaps two brushes with death in as many days had unhinged the Rottweiler. Or, maybe, it was just bored stiff living in Froikham. Most likely, it had been trained by some marijuana-growing local to attack anything wearing a uniform. Whatever the reason, the huge dog came tearing up Froikham High Street, trailing bandages in its wake, like some mummified Hell-hound, then launched itself at the nearest copper. It took all three of his companions to pull 200 pounds of slavering canine off their screaming comrade and wrestle the dog to the ground. Even then, four of them could barely hold the manic pooch, as its rabid jowls sought to wreak havoc on the nearest plod knacks.

The train vanished over the horizon in an oily haze. Doug rolled down the window.

"Ehmm... We'll be going, officers," he announced pleasantly. "Don't be doing anything rude to that dog with your truncheons."

He turned the key in the ignition. The engine coughed and died.

"Ooh," he said.

"What do you mean... Ooh?"

The policemen had begun dragging the squirming Rottweiler towards the railroad tracks, where they spotted a coil of stout rope.

"They're gonna tie the dog to the tracks." We were momentarily distracted. "Nasty fuckers."

"I really urge you to get this car started, Doug."

The policemen's plan had become apparent. They got one end of the rope over the dog's neck and hauled the mammoth hound to the train barrier. With a gargantuan effort, they wound the rope around the striped wood, leapt back from the frantic, slavering animal and grinned at each other. Doug's windscreen wipers began to swish back and forth.

"I'm getting a bit nervous now," he admitted. "I've gone all thumbs."

The policemen started towards us again, thumping batons against their palms.

There was a loud 'ting' behind them as the railroad lights changed from red to green.

Slowly, the barrier began to rise.

Doug tooted his horn and pointed. The policemen turned and looked in the direction he was indicating.

The Rottweiler was dangling, six feet in the air, still tied by its neck to the upright barrier. Its legs flailed wildly above the frosty ground and it wore a look of canine astonishment, even more pronounced than the day before.

"We may have to report you to the R.S.P.C.A," Doug shouted. "I can see the local news headlines now. *Vigilantes in blue lynch defenceless pet. Claim it fell down the stairs in the nick while drunk.*"

"Yeah!" Bob chimed in. "This'll put a big dent in applicants wanting to be police dogs."

The policemen turned and sprinted back to the frantically bobbing Rottweiler.

Doug turned the ignition key and, at last, the Vauxhall's engine sputtered to life. We pulled out from the kerb and drove cautiously over the railway line, past the four policemen dancing around the revolving dog, arms stretched above their heads.

"Wow. Hound Lake." Bob leaned out the window. "Some people pay good money to see that kind of thing."

Standing on tip-toe, the policemen had just enough elevation to support the Rottweiler's massive rump with their fingers and keep it from choking. The dog glared balefully at us as we slid past.

"They've got little veins sticking out on their fore-heads." Bob leaned out the window with a camera.

"That's one for the police gazette boys," he grinned.

Then we drove off into the thickening snow.

We never did get caught. The local constabulary knew who we were, of course, but the whole raid had been such an unmitigated fiasco the authorities preferred to forget it ever happened. All charges were dropped, even against the Muir twins, though they were warned if they tried anything like it again, they would be executed for treason.

Bob still has the photograph after all these years, but you can't really tell what it is because his thumb was in the way.

As for Doug. A couple of weeks later, he went out and bought himself a Rottweiler.

Wasted Trip

When you were a kid, did you ever climb a hill on your own, y'know? Just to lie and look at the sky and wonder what it would be like to be a bird and fly.

If so, you probably didn't have any friends.

When I was a kid, we had potato picking holidays, two weeks in October, before they perfected machines to do it. I passed one driving to my dad's house, chugging up gobbets of frosty mud where there once were lines of arses wreathed in cigarette smoke and condensation.

I don't see my dad much. I left home a long time ago. Cut my roots and shouted timber - I wanted to move, not to grow. So I swapped a lack of shops for a lack of fresh air.

My dad is a lonely man. At least, I assume so because I'm never around to ask. Solid and silent as a turnip, he had planted himself in his living room - though he did recite some Robert Burns to me, the verses of Burns being his passion.

I find that strange. Burns, after all, being a poet of the people, not of the land. He, too, deserted his farm, before he died of a sort of human version of Dutch Elm Disease.

"Aye... Rabbie Burns," my father said. He made it sound like a description.

He brought out some digestive biscuits and started eating them, one after the other. My dad chewed digestives with the kind of concentration that verged on disturbing. Grazing is the word that comes to mind. And it reminded me of a time when I was a kid and went potato picking, so I told him about it.

During my tea break, I'd climbed up this pretty wee wooded hill, a carrot top of Silver Birch, sticking out from the flat tilled land. There, I found a Magic Mushroom carpet right among the sheep. Brilliant, I thought... up here tomorrow lunchtime with a couple of carrier bags. Make myself a fortune.

Of course, I didn't tell my dad that part.

Only, next day, the tattie bus went to another field and I never saw the hill again.

"I'm pregnant, da," I said.

"You're looking for Dunnechin Brae," my father replied. "Just off the B904. You take the Arbroath road."

Well. I'd told him.

On the way back, I turned onto the B904. I didn't recognise it, but then again... 20 years. 20 years since the tattie bus muscled its tired oily carcass over the fields. Windows crusted with grime, interior filled with noxious fumes and mass coughing, gouts of dust erupting from the seat backs with every bump. It was like World War One on wheels.

Anyway, I didn't find Dunnechin Brae. I think I discovered where it might have been, but they were building Barratt houses there and I couldn't get any farther up the road for traffic cones and churned up earth. There was a footpath off to one side, but some workman had wedged a plate glass across it, leaning against two trees. A bunch of sheep had come down the hill and walked right into the glass. Now they had their big, sooty faces pressed against it, staring forlornly at me.

Or maybe Dunnechin Brae only existed in my dad's head.

You know those electric fences you used to get - a wire strand looped through little poles? When I was young and went berry picking, they had one to keep the cows away from the rasps. If you grabbed hold, it nearly jolted your knuckles out of their sockets. Get a wee kid, wet from the bushes, to lean his head on it, and you could practically dislocate his neck.

You wouldn't get away with that now.

Things have changed in the countryside. Genetic horticultural advances, I suppose. I drove past what seemed to be an electrified field on the way home. Barley, I think it was. I could see birds landing, then they'd all bounce back into the air. A few field mice had wandered in as well and, now and then, they'd ping up over the gently waving sheaves.

Boing. Boing. Boing.

I spotted the A23 on the other side of the field, partly obscured by trees and the occasional flying rabbit. If I could get onto it, I would be home in an hour. I stopped at the junction and saw a hawk hovering above me, high in the sky. I got so engrossed in watching I let half a dozen cars go past.

Suddenly it plummeted. It plunged and my heart plunged with it. Whoosh. Straight down.

It got hit by a car a few inches from the ground. Vroooom. Swept away.

I didn't quite know what to think about that. I didn't know quite how I felt either - but I knew it wasn't enough.

In circumstances like these, I have a trick. I imagine my child.

I imagined my child was sitting next to me in the car, and I glanced over to see what its reaction was.

It was looking the other way.

Good job, I guess. I wouldn't have known what to tell it, this imaginary kid. I could explain that the hawk had seen a mouse on the road and swooped down to grab it. Then, it had been annihilated by a much larger, stronger force and that was just the way things were. Or, I could tell him that the hawk, flying high and seeing everything going on below him, had decided to commit suicide.

Problem was... I didn't know which explanation sounded worse.

When I was younger, I took magic mushrooms and they made me hallucinate. I saw strange things and felt strange inside about what I saw. But you know, it wasn't what I felt or what I saw that gave me a thrill. It was the fact that it wasn't real.

See, I don't think anything real is nice. Nothing natural is nice either... it follows from that. I also think there's only one myth left in the world - and it's built into every brick of the city where I live.

It's the myth that we can conquer nature. Both outside, in the universe, and inside - human nature itself. But you can't conquer anything... it just bubbles underneath. Waiting to engulf you.

So, we choose to destroy it.

You know what I believe? I believe it's in our nature to drive around, watching our world being slowly paved over. Looking for a little hill and a crop of something not quite real - one that hasn't been built upon or ploughed under. Something only a bird could spot because, if it hasn't been eradicated, it's still hidden down some forgotten side road in our imagination.

Of course, I didn't tell my dad that part.

Chairman of the Board

If a tree falls in the forest and no one hears it, does it make a sound?

George Berkeley: Anglican bishop and philosopher (1685-1753).

To die will be an awfully big adventure.

J.M. Barrie. *Peter Pan.*

Daler Board Meeting Minutes: 1

"Progress?"

The Chairman of Daler sat at one end of his long boardroom, sunk in a huge leather chair. He was so far away I wondered if he was going to whip out opera glasses to see the product properly.

Popper was at the receiving end of his comment and the focus of everyone's attention. He stood in front of a magnificent wide-screen monitor used for official presentations, which he completely ignored. Popper was never one for showing off.

On a trolley beside him was an unassuming laptop. It was bigger and clumsier than Daler's current best-seller, the *Mamba Striker 7*. That didn't bode well.

"This is the *Weej 13*," Popper said. "It's a quantum leap forward in our technology. Literally."

"He is so fired," Lacy muttered next to me.

"Specifications," the Chairman snapped.

"It incorporates a quantum chip. Very experimental but undeniably promising. There are no raised keys because the keyboard operates using the same principle as those air hockey games you get in an arcade." Popper thought for a moment. "I suppose you'd just call it a board."

"Clunky, isn't it?" I hissed. "That'll make for a hard sell."

"What about connectivity?" Tennyson from Tech raised his hand. "Are there any marked improvements to the HD screen? Don't tell me you brought the headphone jack back?"

"I sacrificed all that stuff to make way for new components."

The board members gasped. Their eyes apprehensively shifted from Popper to the Chairman as if they were watching a tennis match played with a grenade.

"Why?"

I had to admire the Chairman's economy with words. The astonished gazes swung back towards Popper.

"I was well on my way to producing the *Mamba Striker 8* when I discovered a function for this machine that no company can match." He shrugged. "To be honest, I've no idea how I did it. But it works and we can replicate it."

"You can't throw a design that took years to perfect out the window for one new application." Tennyson had obviously appointed himself Devil's advocate. "Marketing will go apeshit."

"Billy and I are marketing," Lacy snorted. "Tenn is right, though. *Weej 13* looks like it was built by Atari. In 1989."

"Explain." The Chairman raised a liver-spotted hand to silence them.

"This isn't a laptop." Popper smiled for the first time. "It's a Ouija Board."

There was an eruption of stifled laughter and groans of embarrassment from the board members. The Chairman cleared his throat noisily and the hubbub immediately stopped. He wasn't known for his patience.

"You say it works."

"And how." Popper patted the machine. "It doesn't just talk to the dead. It summons them. Permanently, as far as I can tell."

"This is ridiculous," Tennyson scoffed. "If you're stuck with the new model, just man up and say so."

"Tell that to my technical research assistant, Marylin," Popper retorted. "She's in the lobby outside."

"Did she come up with this dumb idea?"

"Marylin died of cancer six months ago."

The board sprang up, toppling over chairs. They trooped out, murmuring to each other. Lacy and I were about to join them but the Chairman waved us back down.

"Marketing ideas," he commanded.

"Because of COVID-19, you're probably feeling a bit lost and lonely." Lacy stroked her chin. "Now you can have your family with you all the time. Even if they've passed away."

"Don't let death spoil your social life," I added.

"*Weej 13* is a terrible name, though," Lacy complained. "Sounds like a shaman from Glasgow. What about *Mortal Coil 1*?"

"I like it." The Chairman nodded.

The others shuffled back in, white and shaking.

"I put my hand right through her," Tennyson said. "I don't. I just…"

It was nice to see him lost for words.

"Simms?" The Chairman turned to his Head of Finance. "Give Popper whatever he needs to put this into full production."

"Yes, sir."

Popper smiled again.

Daler Board Meeting Minutes: 2

"Report."

"We've certainly let a cat among the pigeons." Julius from Public Relations had the floor and the screen was filled with charts and graphs, which nobody understood. "Let me start with the good news. Sales have exceeded our wildest expectations. In fact, we're struggling to produce enough *Mortal Coils* to satisfy demand."

"That is not good news and you have no idea what my expectations are. Put all our resources into building more machines."

Coming from the Chairman, this constituted a major speech. Julius was suitably abashed.

"We're calling these 'ghosts' The Re-united. We wanted The Returned but there are a couple of shows on Netflix already using the term and they threatened litigation for copywrite infringement."

"Acceptable," the Chairman grunted.

"Understandably, we've received flak from all major religions. They're less than pleased to find that, no matter which God they believe in, their adherents can bring back loved ones. They're trying to get around it by various counterclaims."

"Such as?"

"Ghosts don't have souls. It's all a mass hallucination." Julius ticked off the excuses on his fingers. "They're not really spirits but beings from another dimension."

"That's an odd claim for religious institutions to make," Tennyson remarked dryly. "A multiverse kind of makes God redundant."

"So does logic," Lacy smirked. "It's all marketing, Tenn."

"My favourite is their idea that the whole thing is a trick by Satan," Julius continued.

All eyes switched to the Chairman but the irony was obviously lost on him. He wasn't known for his sense of humour.

"Officially, we're in the clear," Passmore from legal broke in. "There's no law against what we're selling."

"Our biggest problem is that the Re-united don't seem to *do* much. They kind of hang about the places they're used to, performing the same actions they always did. Don't show a lot of interest in the people who summoned them, neither."

Julius shrugged.

"At the moment, the sheer novelty of having your dead dad around is enough. That may wane with time, I imagine."

"Your loved ones the way you always wanted them." I framed a banner in the air. "No mess. No fuss."

"Billy and I have plenty of advertising ideas, never fear." Lacy exuded confidence, like always.

"As you suggested in your memo," Julius said. "The board has all had a go at resurrecting someone. Now we need some feedback."

A few of the members winced. A suggestion from the Charman was really an order.

"C'mon, folks," Julius urged. "Can't do my job properly if you won't flag any obstacles."

"My mum follows me from room to room," Tennyson said eventually. "She doesn't hassle me or anything, but…"

He lapsed into sullen silence.

"Out with it," the Chairman commanded.

"I've got a Maserati and a penthouse apartment - but how am I supposed to bring a girl home now?" His face reddened. "I can't even… ehm… masturbate with her watching."

"I have the opposite problem," Simms put his head in both hands. "My gran goes at it with a vibrator every day. Four o'clock on the dot."

There was muted sniggering around the table.

"It's not funny," Simms cried. "I've had to go into therapy."

"There is a point I'd like to raise," Lacy said. "My sister and her boyfriend died in a car crash so, naturally, I brought her back."

I raised an eyebrow. I hadn't known about any sister. Then again, Lacy and I were work colleagues rather than friends.

"A few days later, the boyfriend appeared too." Lacy frowned. "They spend all day necking on the couch. And... more."

"There you go," Julius beamed. "Isn't that nice?"

"Lovers Re-united," I gave Lacy a thumbs up. "See what I did there? We could use it as a tagline."

"Only, I didn't bring the boyfriend back," Lacy continued sourly. "I can't imagine who would. He was a violent scumbag everyone but my sister hated. Even his parents disowned him."

"I'll have the research department look into that." Julius blanched. Then he reluctantly asked the question on all our minds.

"Did... eh... you partake in the experiment, Sir?" He bit his lip nervously. "Perhaps you'd like to share your experience."

"I only look to the future," the Chairman said evenly. "The dead are has-beens."

Daler Board Meeting Minutes: 3

"Where is Simms?" the Chairman demanded.

The board members fidgeted awkwardly in their seats and glanced at an empty chair.

"Simms committed suicide," Tennyson said finally. "I guess he didn't like his grandmother as much as he thought."

"Then why isn't he here?"

"Good point, sir." Bertram from Personnel made a quick note. "I'll draw up his dismissal papers."

Poor old Simms. Now he was dead, stuck with his horny gran and out of a job. He never was one for thinking things through.

"Continue," the Chairman folded bony hands on his chest.

Popper had the floor. The man's face was pale from lack of sleep and his dishevelled hair was sticking up as if he had seen a ghost. Which was more than likely, under the circumstances. Come to think of it, the entire board was looking worse for wear.

"The Re-united appear to be acclimatising to life among the living," Popper said glumly. "It looks like they've started bringing back their own loved ones, whether the device's owner likes it or not."

"Didn't you include password protection?" The Chairman's face was granite.

"It's hard to hide stuff like that when a dead person is always looking over your shoulder. A lot of customers are trying to return the machines before their warranty expires."

"Got that covered," the Head of Marketing assured us. "*Mortal Coil* does exactly what it's meant to. No refunds."

"Excellent."

"It's getting rather disturbing, though," Popper said. "My dad brought back his dad, who brought back his dad... and so on." He wiped his brow. "I found a Nazi in the garden shed and a Victorian gardener trying to dig up my rose bushes."

"Projections?" The Chairman was not known for his sympathetic nature.

"Roughly 15 times as many people have died in the past as are living now. If this carries on, the world is going to get very crowded. Add in the animals and...

"Animals?"

"Dogs and cats, mainly. But there have been reports of bison on the streets of Chicago. I presume some expired medicine man is behind that."

"I'm loath to do anything so drastic." Tennyson hesitated. "But I feel we may have to consider a recall."

"I second that," Lacy added belligerently. "I've got a Roman Centurion on my toilet."

"I don't think it matters," Popper said quietly. "I'm pretty sure the Re-united have learned to bring back folk from the other side without the need for technology."

"That's an infringement of our patents." The Chairman's eyes blazed. "How do we get rid of them?"

"I don't know."

"Figure it out!" Tennyson urged. "We're already facing some major class-action lawsuits."

"It's worse than that," Popper replied. "Folk can see what it's like to be dead and they're none too pleased by the revelation. People are turning to atheism in their millions."

"Positives?" The Chairman demanded.

"Well, wars have almost stopped because nobody is willing to die anymore," Julius said. "Except Simms, apparently."

"That's not a positive," the Chairman grunted. "We have an armaments division."

"No, Sir. Sorry, Sir." Julius shot Popper an anguished glance. "Perhaps we could reverse the polarity on the machine?"

"This isn't an episode of fucking *Star Trek*, Julius. I'm working on it."

"Miss McPherson?" It was the first time the Chairman had ever used Lacy's name. He must be desperate.

"I can't see any spin that will work in these circumstances," Lacy admitted. "We're up shit creek without a canoe, never mind a paddle and our stocks are sinking."

"Disappointing." The Chairman pursed his lips, managing to give everyone the evil eye at once. "I don't pay you to fail."

"No," Lacy shot back. "You're paying us to take the blame for *your* failure. I'm not some inverse exorcist and I do my job bloody well."

There was a shocked hush. Julius almost slid under the table.

"Hmmmmm. If you want something done right, do it yourself." The Chairman got slowly to his feet. "All right. I shall be back once I've sorted this."

He walked, ramrod straight, to the window and slid it open.

"In the meantime, Miss McPherson is in charge."

"Me?" Lacy stammered. "Why?"

"You're the only person who ever dared contradict me."

Then he jumped.

We ran to the window and peered out. The Chairman was a crumpled speck on the sidewalk, twenty floors below. He wasn't known for his ability to take criticism.

"Give the man his due," I whistled. "He put his money where his mouth is."

At the moment, his mouth was probably somewhere at the back of his skull, but I felt that would be taking the analogy a tad far.

"Get on the *Mortal Coil* and bring him back," Julius urged Popper. "See if he has any answers."

"What's the point?" Popper was shaking. "He's going to be like the rest of them."

"He's the Chairman," Julius objected. "Nothing stops that bastard getting what he wants."

"We'll wait a few hours." Lacy stopped the argument with a raised finger. "Give him time to find some answers."

"You're the boss." Popper shut the laptop.

"Yes," Lacy grinned. "Yes, I am."

I shuddered.

Daler Board Meeting Minutes: 4

"Report."

Lacy sat in the Chairman's leather seat, wearing an expensive chiffon jacket. It felt strange not having my only confidant next to me. The other board members seemed bone-weary and dispirited. Bertram was wearing pyjamas with bunny slippers and looked like he'd had them on for several days. There was an egg stain down the front of his dressing gown.

"We found the Chairman." Popper was close to tears. "He's in his mansion out on the West Key. Spends most of his time trying to do a jigsaw puzzle he can't touch and shouting at the staff. Doesn't seem to realise they all quit."

"Sales?"

"Non-existent."

"Legal status?"

"Now we're being sued by the right-to-life mob." Passmore heaved a sigh. "We've got Neanderthals and mammoths running around but no dead fetuses. They claim we're hiding them in Guantanamo Bay."

I noticed Passmore had grown a beard. It might have been a disguise, as the board were getting daily threats on their lives. Perhaps, he didn't see the point in shaving anymore.

"We're fighting lawsuits brought about by The Christian League, who are horrified by the fact that they found Jesus and he looks like a Palestinian. Plus the Arab states, the World Health Organisation, the American society for Psychics, The Proud Boys and Donald Trump, to name but a few."

"Donald Trump?"

"He claims the dead voted against him illegally."

"Yeah, but that was after the elect... Aw, never mind." Lacy closed her eyes wearily.

"There's also a jihad out on all board members but, thankfully, not many takers. World religions have well and truly lost their appeal with the populace."

"Summation?"

There was silence from the board. Bertram produced a pair of needles and began to knit.

"We are well and truly fucked?" I volunteered.

"Put out a press release." Lacy patted her cheeks and let out a huge sigh. "Say we are days off finding a way to return the Re-united to whence they came."

"You really want to use the word *whence*?" Tennyson asked. "It's old-fashioned."

"I don't give a shit how you phrase it." Lacy stood up. "We'll find a way around the problem. We always do. And at the next meeting, I want you all groomed and in suits."

She put on her overcoat.

"Meeting adjourned. I need a triple vodka and Coke. Usual place, if anyone cares to join me."

The board began packing away their things.

"You too, Popper," Lacy commanded. "Bring your research. We need to pick your brains."

"I do have some ideas," Popper sighed. "Normally I'm not much of a drinker but, tonight, I'll make an exception."

We sat in the local bar. A couple of shady characters were playing pool and there was a collection of mountain men skinning beaver in one corner.

"I don't get it," Tennyson complained. "These ghosts are incorporeal. Why don't they sink into the earth or fly off into space?"

"Death, like life, is full of unanswered questions," Bertram said philosophically.

"Whatevs. If we've no idea where these bastards came from, how can we send them back?" Tennyson raised a middle digit to the mountain men. "I'm not sure Popper is up to the task."

"I'm right next to you, dumbass," Popper slurred, waving to the barman. "Another whisky and pineapple, please."

"Settle down, Pops," Lacy grunted. "Let's hear your words of wisdom."

I was tired of the whole thing, so I made my excuses and left. Just like last time.

That's what saved my life.

A car bomb demolished the building five minutes later. About twenty different organisations claimed they were behind it. Except Donald Trump, who denied all responsibility.

Phelps from Homeland Security was waiting for me as I left the bar.

"Any luck, Billy?"

"I didn't learn anything about how to send the Re-united back. But I took minutes like you asked."

"You were part of the team who developed *Mortal Coil*." Phelps' displeasure was palpable. "I thought you might have some insight we missed."

"For the hundredth time, I was in the marketing department. They'll repeat the same actions, over and over, until they die again. Send in a whole squad of agents for the next round, if you want. The board won't notice."

Then I had a thought.

"Didn't you get hold of Popper's research?"

"It's encrypted and his handwritten notes went up in the blast." Phelps sighed. "His ghost carries them around in a folder but, of course, we can't open the damned thing."

He shook my hand.

"I guess you kept your end of the bargain. You're free to go."

He glanced around.

"Wow. Is that a velociraptor?"

I walked back to my house, as it was a beautiful night. The streets were packed with partygoers, though I couldn't tell which were dead and which alive. There was a group of ranch hands practising their quick draw on 21st Avenue but they might have been in fancy dress. Not that it mattered. In the city, almost everyone is a stranger.

No cars, though, which was nice. Drivers didn't want to plough through a bunch of phantoms and discover they'd mown down a real pedestrian in the process. The air smelt clean for a change.

When I got home, I made myself some dinner and sat between my parents.

"Did you know?" I said. "The Aztecs made swords embedded with prismatic obsidian that are far sharper than present-day razor blades? Or Ancient Egypt had proctologists called 'shepherds of the anus'? That Mayans cultivated stingless bees in Central America and the Indus Valley Civilisation had the world's earliest known flush toilets?"

They didn't seem interested in my revelations but no surprise there. They never had. Also, they died in 1996.

"It's amazing what you can learn these days just by observing."

Because I *had* been observing. Well… snooping. It's a trait of mine. For instance, when Popper was still alive, I'd snuck into his office and had a peek at his notes.

But I'd no intention of telling Phelps from Homeland Security what Popper had written on the last page.

One of the most bizarre premises of quantum theory states that, by the very act of watching, the observer affects observed reality.

"The board were looking at this all wrong," I told mum and dad. "The Re-united haven't come from anywhere. They were always here. We just couldn't see them."

"Would you like some melted cheese on toast?" Mum asked dad.

"Yes, dear, I would."

"It's simple quantum physics," I continued. "*The Mortal Coil 1* didn't summon anyone. It just made them visible to those who are alive."

I patted my mother's knee affectionately and my hand slid through to the couch. Still, it was nice having them around again. My wife would be home soon, too. She'd ignore me, of course. The fact that she was still alive wouldn't change that.

It's about acceptance in the end. All in all, I was quite satisfied with how the world was turning out and saw no need to alter it. That was the problem with corporate types and government departments. They couldn't stand change unless they were controlling it.

"You want the problem to stop existing?" I shrugged. "Shut your fucking eyes."

I got up, fetched myself a glass of wine and sat down again.

"I can't believe nobody gets that. After all, it's what we always do."

Then again, people are not known for their common sense.

The Camera Never Lies

Each Sunday, Zuzanna fed the pigeons from a bench in the Rynek Główny.

The birds knew when she was coming, swooping across St Mary's Basilica or rising in waves from the other side of the square. Settling around her, they pecked and squabbled, a hungry riot of grey.

"Calm down, you babies," she snapped in mock annoyance, for they made her feel wanted and she was slightly ashamed of that.

Stallholders in the Cloth Hall chattered and shouted, holding up wooden dolls and fur hats, while the smell of oscypek drifted across from a nearby stand. Her stomach rumbled and she ate a slice of the bread she had brought. The pigeons glared at her effrontery and angrily bobbed tufted heads. Two officers of the Esbecja strolled past, one kicking out at the feathered mob.

199

Zuzanna turned away.

The men paid her no heed. Long black hair, descending from a woollen bobble hat, hid her face and a large, shapeless coat obscured the rest of her body.

She spotted a middle-aged man, several yards away, struggling with a metal tripod. Each time he set it up, then tried to attach his camera, it fell over. The man did not curse or get annoyed. He simply bent down and tried again.

"He's a lot more patient than you," she scolded the pigeons, some of whom were trying to scramble onto her lap.

When the tripod collapsed for the fourth time, she got up and went to help.

"Here you are." She righted the apparatus. "Do you want me to put the camera on as well?"

"You speak English." The stranger sounded surprised.

"I'm a teacher," she replied, as if that explained everything. "And you are American."

"Spotted the accent, huh?"

Zuzanna was tempted to point out she knew his nationality because the jacket he wore would cost her a month's salary - and the camera looked even more expensive.

"Thank you but I'll manage," the man said. "Appreciate the help, though."

Zuzanna nodded politely and returned to her bench. Realising the food was gone, the birds began to slowly disperse. She took out a book and pretended to read.

The man had given up and was strolling towards her. She ignored him and went back to her novel.

"Name's James H. Robinson." He sat down, uninvited. "I'm on vacation. My wife passed away and I had to take early retirement. Got bored and decided to travel a bit."

And you picked Krakow? Zuzanna was curious despite herself. She had no wish to engage the man in conversation yet felt she should warn him.

"You leave that tripod over there and someone will steal it."

"Can't really use the damned thing anymore." James Robinson held up his hand and they both watched it quiver. "Turns out I have a genetic disorder and it's getting worse. I was a professional photographer, so it's put a bit of a spanner in my work."

Americans. Zuzanna thought. *Always brash, talkative and quick to point out their problems. He'll be telling me his life story next.*

"Sorry to hear that," she replied brusquely, wishing the man would go away.

"I was in Krakow once before," Robinson continued as if on cue. "1945. War correspondent, attached to a Russian battalion, when we were still tentative allies. Changed my life, it did."

"The war changed everyone's life." Zuzanna was finding it increasingly difficult to be civil. "More so, if you lived here."

It was the year her mother and father had died.

"I took a picture that became famous right in this square." Robinson waved his hand around. "Only one that ever did. Been living off the proceeds ever since."

Rather than answer, Zuzanna turned her collar up to combat the hostile wind.

"It appeared in newspapers all over the world." he laughed. "Guess I'm back to relive my brief moment of glory."

Zuzanna felt a flush of shame. The man wasn't boasting. He was lonely.

Then the Esbecja returned, curious and drawn to an obvious stranger. Robinson fumbled with his camera, pointed it at them and took a picture.

"Don't do that." The woman tried to shield the lens with her hand. "Those are secret police."

"I didn't think they were parking attendants. But it's a good shot."

"What are you up to?" one officer demanded, pulling the peak of his cap down.

"I'm not doing any harm," Robinson objected, camera shaking.

"Then, why are you so scared?" the policeman sneered, holding out his hand. "Give that to me right now."

"It's a free country, isn't it?" Robinson took another shot.

He may be dumb, Zuzanna thought. *But he certainly isn't short of courage.*

"Give it here," the man repeated, unclipping the holster on his belt.

Zuzanna groaned and jumped up, heart thudding in her chest.

"What do you want to go bothering him for?" she snapped in Polish, "He's a crazy American tourist. Probably thinks he's in Disneyland and you're wearing costumes."

Robinson was still shooting, so she got between him and his aggressors.

"I'll take care of it. Where's your sense of hospitality?"

The man lowered his camera, eyes wide.

"Very well. But he takes one more picture of me and I'll stick this costumed boot up his ass. Tell him that."

The men laughed to each other and walked away.

Zuzanna sat back down, trembling as much as Robinson, slowly letting out her breath. The American was staring at her. He pulled a small square from his pocket.

"This was the picture I took in 1945."

It showed a teenager with bobbed blonde hair standing up to two armed and menacing Russian soldiers, terrified but defiant. The photograph was immensely powerful. Instantly iconic.

"She was protecting me from a couple of thugs in uniform, who… eh… objected to my capturing them on film." Robinson lowered his voice. "When I looked through the viewfinder just now, I realised that girl was you."

He gave an astonished chuckle.

"The camera never lies."

"Correct, I'm sorry to say," Zuzanna grunted. "Stalin did not appreciate the image, as you can imagine. I had to die my hair and go to college in a different town."

Robinson looked abashed.

"I've come to terms with it, but don't think I'm going to make a habit of saving your inconsiderate hide every twenty-five ye…"

She stopped in mid-flow as Robinson took her picture again.

"S*eriously?*"

"Here's a sobering thought." He placed the camera on his lap before it dropped from his grasp. "I owe my success to you and perhaps my life. But also the overwhelming sense that I'm a complete failure."

"What am I getting the blame for now?"

"I'm really not that good at my job," Robinson stated matter-of-factly. "Was gonna quit until you came along. Then, I caught the face every photographer dreams about at the perfect moment. Never came close to capturing that magic again."

He looked dazed.

"Until now."

"All the same, I'd rather you didn't use the picture," Zuzanna said wearily. "I'm too old to start over."

"Me too." Robinson tucked away the photograph. "Anyway, I'm retired and supposed to be on vacation. Keep the camera and tripod. They're worth a fair bit."

He patted her shoulder.

"Happy to sign my future royalties over, too. I'm well enough off and got no kids of my own."

"Then I better stick close in case you start an international incident around the next corner." Zuzanna helped Robinson to his feet. "Would you perhaps like to have lunch?"

"I'd be honoured."

"Good, because you're paying." She winked at him. "Save some for the pigeons."

The Great Pompydoo

The Great Pompydoo was the best singer in the world. That's why his records sold millions, even though he never gave concerts or interviews.

I asked my mother once why that was. After all, she knew him.

Mum said maybe it was cause the Great Pompydoo had a great secret. Then she looked a bit sad.

The Great Pompydoo came to visit us twice a year. My dad runs a little recording studio near Ullapool, on the west coast of Scotland. It's in the middle of no-where but that's why the Great Pompydoo uses it. He says it's his only chance for some real peace and quiet and, of course, my mother is an old friend.

Twice a year, the Great Pompydoo would sit with mum in our garden, both drinking brightly coloured drinks in tall glasses and watching the sun sink behind the mountains. They grew up poor in the same village in Spain, my mother told me, and everyone thought they would end up together. But the Great Pompydoo had gone off to seek his fortune and mum had married my father instead.

My mother is extremely beautiful and the Great Pompydoo is very handsome. My father is funny and kind, but he is also short, podgy and balding. I love my dad, but I'm glad I look like my mum.

Once night fell, the Great Pompydoo and my father would go to dad's recording studio and the Great Pompydoo would record another million-selling album. The next day, his chauffer would whisk him off in a big pink Cadillac. A month later, my father would receive a cheque. I don't know how much, but it was enough that we could afford a nice house and dad never had to look for any other customers.

As for me, I liked living in the highlands. There were trees to climb, bays and hills to explore and two or three kids in a nearby village to hang out with. Not a bad place to grow up, I guess. But I wasn't entirely happy.

Just like the Great Pompydoo, I had a secret.

And I was afraid our secret might be the same.

One Saturday, when the sun was shining and the air was still, I went to Inchmurry Cove and sat on the beach. It's one of my favourite places, because there's a half-moon of cliffs around the small inlet that gives the whole place a natural echo. Wonderful acoustics.

So, I began to sing.

See, I want desperately to be a singer. But I can't let anyone hear my voice.

That is part of *my* great secret.

Here on the deserted beach, I was completely alone and so I belted out *I Better Leave Right Now* by Will Young. Why not? I can perform it better than him. I was just getting to the warbly bit I like when a shadow fell across the rock I was sitting on.

I jerked around, my heart thumping.

Mother and father stood behind me, holding hands. They must have been out walking on the beach. My mum was staring at me, mouth open, and my dad had tears in his eyes.

"I didn't know you could sing like that," he breathed. "You sound exactly like...."

His voice trailed off and he glanced at my mother.

"Like the Great Pompydoo," she said quietly.

I bowed my head. I didn't know what to say. I knew who I sounded like and it made me afraid and confused. My father looked sadly out to sea. Then he sat beside me and placed a hand gently on my shoulder. My mother knelt on the other side.

"There's something we have to tell you," she said. "It's *our* great secret."

"The Great Pompydoo is a very private man," dad continued. "He never really wanted to be famous and have people treat him differently. He just wanted to sing, make a bit of money and live in peace with his family."

Mum pulled a crumpled magazine from her bag and smoothed it out. On the cover was the Great Pompydoo, smiling his dazzling smile. She tapped the cover.

"This man's real name is Raoul Catillana," she said. "As you know, I grew up with him. People said we were bound to marry one day."

I nodded, still afraid to look at my father. My mother leaned close and whispered in my ear.

"I didn't want to." She leaned back and winked at me. "You want to know what Raoul Catalina's great secret is."

I shook my head.

"He can't sing a note."

"But... but, he's the Great Pompydoo!"

"Raoul Catalina craved riches and fame." My father laughed and his stomach wobbled. "I just wanted to sing."

"Raoul and I will always be good friends," my mother smiled. "But I fell for a man who knew that my love was more precious than being important."

She squeezed my father's hand.

"Well. Go on!" she urged. "Show our son who you are."

And my father began to sing. He had the most beautiful voice in the world. I should know. I'd heard it on a dozen million-selling albums.

My mother took my hand, eyes glistening, and nodded for me to join in. After a while I did, timidly at first, but my father grinned and motioned for me to keep going.

And we sang together, on the beach, in front of my mum. The first of many times.

Singing the way people do, who have no more secrets between them.

Hobnobble

The woman sat on the steps, under one of the George Square statues, wearing a simple black and white dress. The woman, not the statue. It occurred to her that she didn't even know who the graven image was. She'd led too sheltered a life, she thought. That's why she'd bought a newspaper today. Above her, torn ribbons of cloud fluttered in the summer breeze. She put her hands together and stared up at the beautiful blue sky.

Out of the corner of her eye, she saw a figure approach. He was average height, with an average face, and wearing a shabby grey raincoat.

The woman looked down at her purse, uncertain whether to pull it closer or fish out some loose change for him. As the unkempt figure reached her, he gave a little hopping dance, then pirouetted daintily. From a few steps below, he grinned and gave a small bow.

"Tah dah!"

The woman stared at him. He didn't look particularly threatening. He gave another hop and almost lost his balance.

"Tah dah!"

He pursed thin lips and blew a raspberry, gurning maniacally. The woman slid the purse behind her. The stranger tried a few tentative bodybuilding poses but it didn't look quite right, what with his scrawny physique and him wearing a Mac. Then he strutted around for a bit, making growling noises.

The woman kept staring. She didn't know what else to do.

"Rowwrrrrrrr... rowwrrrr... row.." The man stopped suddenly and lowered both hands to his side.

"I'm a demon," he announced.

The woman smiled and nodded. She really wished he would go away.

"No. I mean, I'm a real demon. A demon, demon. Not using this as a figure of speech, you understand. I'm using it in a literal sense. A demon. I'm a demon."

She tried to ignore him. After a few Satanic style lunges, the stranger stopped and rethought his position.

"Oh, for God's sake," he said finally and ran a hand down his face. The nondescript countenance vanished immediately and a scarlet, puffy-faced monster glared at her over the frayed collar of the raincoat. Curling ridged horns protruded from his forehead and his baleful eyes were black as an eight ball.

The woman gave a start.

"Holy shit!"

"S'not pretty, is it?" The creature's words were a bit muffled, for dirty fangs now protruded from inside his bottom lip. With a sigh, he ran a hand back up his face and the harmless, all too human visage, was back.

"You all right?" he asked sheepishly.

The woman blinked rapidly.

"Not really."

"Sorry, sorry. I'm sorry. I was hoping you might, I don't know.... eh... sense my... um... demonicness? Eh? I could tell you're a nun, even without your clothes on. I mean, without your habit on. I didn't mean without your clothes on."

He shuffled awkwardly on the spot.

"You're taking this very well."

The woman swallowed hard, trying to come to terms with what she had seen.

"How come you don't look like that all the time?" she said after a while, wishing she had a can of Mace.

"Come on. It's fine for scaring folk - but try hailing a taxi when you've got a face like a Mandrill's arse." The stranger opened his arms gregariously. "You look a bit peaky yourself."

"I never thought I'd live to see evil incarnate in the flesh."

"Aw, that's very flattering, but I'm hardly evil incarnate in the flesh. Sheesh." The stranger put his hands behind his back and tried to look modest. "I'm just a plain old angel, fallen, of course. Above me, you got your Archangels, Principalities, Powers and above that Virtues and Dominions, The Order of Thrones,

Cherubim and finally Seraphim. Lucifer is one of the Seraphim. I'm just in charge of Glasgow."

The man glanced around and lowered his voice.

"Mammon, my immediate boss, he's in charge of England. He's a Virtue. There's no particular demon for Scotland though. It just gets divided up. I don't know if that will change when you get independence."

He puffed out his scrawny chest.

"Now Astaroth, he's in charge of the USA," he gloated. "And he's not only Order of Thrones, third highest in the hierarchy of demons, but also grand treasurer of hell. We had great hopes for the USA when Trump was in charge," he added in a confidential whisper.

The woman frowned.

"What does hell need a treasurer for?"

"I'm not entirely sure. It's not like we get any wages."

"And you said, *For God's Sake*."

"To be honest, hell isn't all that well run," the demon said thoughtfully. "I mean, it's not like Amazon or anything."

"Is a demon taking the Lord's name in vain the same as a person doing it?" The woman's puzzlement overcame her fear. "I'm confused."

But the stranger had gone off at a tangent.

"I did a Welcome Host course once in the body of a dental receptionist," he mused. "The Happy Zoo theory of management sort of fitted hell. Not very efficient but everybody pitches in, excuse the pun."

The woman straightened her shoulders and struggled to her feet.

"I'm not afraid, you know." She said, trying to keep the quiver from her voice.

The demon seemed lost in his own thoughts.

"Hell doesn't even have a mission statement," he complained.

The woman put down her handbag and took up a karate stance.

"I'm prepared to defend myself, you vile spawn of Satan."

"Yeah, yeah. You can arm wrestle me back into the pit later." The creature grinned and put his arm around her. "I actually came to ask for help."

"You'll not fool me easily, fiend."

"For God's sake, a minute ago, I couldn't convince you I was a demon in the first place."

"Will you stop saying 'For God's sake'? It doesn't seem right."

"Quite so. Best be civil till we figure out what's what, eh?"

"I won't listen to your honeyed words." The woman pointed at him defiantly.

"The name's Hobnobble." He shook the proffered digit.

"Hobnobble?"

"Yes, yes. It's the curse of many a demon. Phizzog worse than a Tusker's scrotum and a name that sounds like a pack of biscuits. And you are?"

"Norma," she said, taken aback.

"Oh, well that makes me feel better." He let go of her finger and licked his palm. "Now, Norman. What do I want from you? You'll like this. I want you to teach me how to be good."

The woman's lips pursed in disapproval.

"Excuse me?"

"I want to be good! Help old ladies across the road instead of changing the traffic lights when they're in the middle. Don't get me wrong, they both seem equally pointless. That's my problem here. I mean, I know the theories. I did a course of ethics disguised as a philosophy student."

He looked suddenly guilty.

"The lectures started at nine in the morning, though. I only went to three."

"Demons can't be good," the woman protested.

"Course we can." Hobnobble looked hurt. "We're the ones started off as angels, remember?"

He gave a terse shrug.

"We do what we're told. Well, that's not fair, really. We're sort of champions of the underdog. Natural revolutionaries, that's the best way to describe demons. Demons are the little guys. Only big."

Norma looked warily at him.

"What do you want?"

"I wanna switch sides."

"Switch sides?"

"Basically."

"Why?"

Hobnobble sat down next to her.

"That's a wee bit embarrassing."

Norma was intrigued, despite herself.

"Try me," she said.

"God's losing."

"Losing."

"Yeah."

"The Almighty."

"He's getting trounced if the truth be known."

"God, the all-seeing, all-knowing and all-powerful." She couldn't keep the sarcasm from her voice, even though she knew it was a sin. Or was it? She couldn't quite remember.

Hobnobble patted her arm condescendingly.

"It was a good line and it served him well, I don't deny it. But it's not just the Devil, you know. Man likes his freedom. Scotland's nuts for it right now. I honestly think you could put a lot of blame on *Braveheart* for that. Ever see it?"

"I don't believe you." Norma insisted.

"Anyway, a whole bunch of us demons have got to go back to fighting for God again. Not my idea. And where to start? Jesus. I mean, *I'm* out of practice."

"You expect me to believe this?" The woman shook her head and narrowed pretty brown eyes.

"You don't?

"Well... Duh!" she raised an eyebrow.

"Yes, that's hell for you." Hobnobble gave a theatrical sigh. "*Let's just tell her the truth*, I said. *As long as you get a result.*"

He shook his head.

"Oh, you should have seen the looks of mortification! Poncing about with their pitchforks going *Oh, fine... God gets to work in mysterious ways but we've got to be Joe Fucking Bricklayer about everything.*"

He stuck out his bottom lip petulantly.

"We're not held in chains down there, you know... its red bloody tape. Look."

He ran up a few steps and spread his arms wide to indicate George Square. "Let's imagine you and I are Adam and Eve. In the Garden of Eden."

Norma had never seen George Square compared to the Garden of Eden before. It was a bit paved. And too many drunk people.

"Right?" Hobnobble continued unfazed. "And we're both bollock naked."

Norma narrowed her eyes again.

"Sorry," Hobnobble apologised once more. "Force of habit. Habit. Get it? Anyway. Garden of Evil, right?

"Eden."

"Yeah. Eden. So. What went wrong? A couple of apples and it's sorry folks, no fig leaves in the GoE. Collect your bearskins on the way out."

"Tempted by a demon." Norma pointed out.

"C'mon, you were straight off the boat. Point is, what did your ancestors do? Ate from some tree, that's all." He licked his lips with a forked tongue. "That was my original argument, too."

"The tree of the knowledge of good and evil." Norma felt bound to drive home the significance of this particular plant. But Hobnobble seemed in agreement.

"Aye. And out you go into the wilderness, in a state of disgrace, and man's history is mong toast from that point. Well... we helped," he added cheerfully.

Norma grunted, but Hobnobble was on a roll.

"And *that's* your original sin."

"Cast into the wilderness," she agreed sadly.

"Forever in a state of disgrace, in the Lord's eyes."

"Congratulations on a job well done."

"I'll come to the point." Hobnobble spotted the sarcasm.

"Please do."

"Right." He indicated the two of them with a slim, manicured finger. "Here we are 6,000 years later."

"6,000 years?"

"Aye. Don't believe all that dinosaur shite." He began to count on his fingers. Norma noticed that they were nicotine stained. At least, she hoped it was nicotine.

"What've we got now? Eh? Global dissatisfaction. The western world doesn't know its arse from Nebuchadnezzar's nipples. Eastern hordes, they still worship Ally Goombah or something – what's *that* all about?"

Norma was a little taken aback.

"You mean the Christian God really is the one true God?" she said.

"Course he is."

"Wow."

Hobnobble put both hands on his hips.

"Not you as well!"

"What do you mean?"

"I mean, we got a planet filled with doubt," he snorted. "Nobody knowing what's really good or bad or right or wrong anymore." He wagged a finger disapprovingly. "Where's a world like that headed?"

Norma shrugged. "Eternal damnation?"

"That's a nice thought," Hobnobble said wistfully. Then his face darkened.

"But no. No!" he roared. "You're headed back towards a fucking state of grace, of course!"

A couple of neds stopped at the commotion and glared at him. Hobnobble shut one eye and pulled down the other. Right to his top lip. The neds blanched and continued on their way. Norma closed one eye as well.

"Run that past me again," she said doubtfully.

Hobnobble leaned over her like a parent explaining curfew times to a difficult teenager.

"Before... you ate from the tree of good and evil..." He slowed down his voice as if he were talking to an idiot. "Mmmmm? Yum, yum...."

Just in case he hadn't insulted Norma enough, he made miming motions to accompany his baby talk.

"You weren't supposed to know anything about anything. See?"

"No."

"No?" Hobnobble sighed loudly. "Well. None of that has changed! You're not supposed to know what's right. What's wrong. That God is good. That the Devil is bad. And you're never going to be in grace with your Lord until you go back to not knowing the difference!"

His eyes flashed.

"Problem is, in this fucked up world full of Christian hypocrites, who refuse to practise what God preaches and use the Bible as their own personal bigot manual, mankind is perilously close to achieving that goal again! We thought inventing science might sort you out, but it's just made things worse. The Big Bang? Quantum Physics? Who the fuck can get their head around that?"

The outburst had turned him an alarming shade of red. Which was actually close to his natural colour, Norma thought.

She wasn't giving in so easily, though.

"That can't be right," she insisted.

"Lady!" Hobnobble almost exploded. "Before you considered leaving your order, you were one of the few people left on this earth who still had unshakeable faith in a good God and a bad Devil. What do you think of them apples? And you're right, of course. God *is* good and the Devil is a total naj... I ought to know."

Hobnobble sank to his knees and clasped his hands in front of his chest.

"So you... you got to *stay* a nun," he pleaded. "See, if enough people still believe that God is good and stick to his principles. Well, then... my lot are always going to be in business."

Norma's eyes widened.

"Wait, wait, wait!" she spluttered.

"You don't believe me?"

"I didn't say that!"

Hobnobble shrugged. "I know you holy rollers aren't big on logic but *think* about it."

"Wait." Norma screwed her eyes shut and concentrated. "So... if man isn't supposed to know the difference between good and evil... then he's not supposed to know God is good."

"Right."

"So everyone should stop worshipping him and turn away from their faith."

"Yup."

"Including me."

"Definitely."

"Or the human race can never return to its state of grace."

"Bingo."

"But it's too late. I already know you're evil. You are evil, aren't you?"

Hobnobble grinned.

"It's a fucker, isn't it?"

"But, if you're evil, you wouldn't want to clarify things unless... you actually wanted me to stay a nun."

"Right,"

"So, if I stay a nun, then you've won cause you got what you wanted. But, eh... if you're lying, then why appear and try dissuading me when I was ready to give it all up?"

"Why indeed?"

"You're not helping!" Norma stamped a dainty foot.

"I'm supposed to?"

"Yet, if I abandon my faith, then I'm damned and you've won again."

"In a nutshell."

For the first time, Norma felt afraid. She began to back down the steps. Unbidden, an old prayer sprang into her head.

"Though I walk through the valley of death," she chanted. "I will fear no evil."

"Now you're getting it," Hobnobble snickered. "I'm on your side, remember? Whichever you choose."

"Our father who art in heaven. Hallowed be thy name..." Norma made the sign of the crucifix.

"Hey, lady, I don't like people to cross me." Hobnobble waved his arms comically at her. "Now get thee to a nunnery."

He opened up his Mac.

"Cause this is what happens to those who take the Lord's name in vain."

Norma's eyes widened. She gave a small shriek, then turned and fled.

Hobnobble watched her go until she vanished into a cloud of startled pigeons.

"Hopefully, you just can't kick that habit. Or those doubts. Either way, I'm fine with it."

He sat down on the steps and pulled a cigarette, already lit, from behind his ear.

"That's the problem with religious types," he muttered to the empty sky.

"They take everything so literally."

Morgan Spurlock

Check this. Morgan Spurlock got famous by eating nothing but McDonalds for a month. So I'm gonna top that by drinking only sea water. I mean, it's still H20, right?

Day 1. Hah. Too easy.

Day 2. Mouth dry but basically fine.

Day 3. Tongue feels like a skunk's bum on heat.

Day 4. So bloody thirsty. Head is pounding. Maybe if I drank more?

Day 5. Ate a watermelon I found in the sea. Tasted like jellyfish.

Day 6. I can see Morgan Spurlock calling to me from the briny depths! He's a mermaid!

I must go to him.

The God Complex

In physics, the 'Observer Effect' is the theory that the mere observation of a phenomenon inevitably changes that phenomenon. This is often the result of instruments that, by necessity, alter the state of what they measure, in some manner.

The Holy Grail is traditionally thought to be the cup Christ drank from at the Last Supper and that Joseph of Arimathea used to collect Jesus's blood at his crucifixion. There are roughly 200 alleged Grail cups in various locations around the world.

Jensen and Murphy peered through the smoked glass partition. On the other side, a dumpy, middle-aged woman sat at her console. She had unusually dark hair, short and permed, with a purple butterfly clasp fastened to one side. It looked remarkably like a wig.

"We call this part of the facility The God Complex," Jensen said dryly. "That's a pun."

Murphy sighed.

Of the pair, Jensen was taller and thinner. He had a clipboard under one arm and was wearing a white lab coat. He looked so much the typical scientist, Murphy wondered if the man had ever considered becoming anything else. Murphy, on the other hand, resembled an Irish bricklayer - short, squat and ginger - and the name didn't help.

He squinted through the window at the woman. She was wearing a gold badge that said *Edith* in small black letters. With a handle like that, it was no surprise she was middle-aged, Murphy thought. Edith had a small microphone on the desk in front of her and was talking into it. Two wires, one red and one white, wound from the back of her head into a bank of steel panels set in the roof.

"It's really quite fascinating." Jensen's voice was slow and emotionless as if he mentally read over everything before saying it. "It's almost like you... plug yourself in. You...plug yourself in, yes. Plug yourself into the computer."

"And you can see what's going on in the past?" Murphy asked.

"You see, yes. No. Yes," Jensen replied hesitantly. "You... experience. You... You... Yes, you see, in a way. Sort of."

Murphy sighed again. He had long ago given up expecting straight answers from anyone in authority. Jensen turned a dial on the panel beside him and the woman's voice suddenly became audible. She sounded like she'd been smoking since she was twelve. Continuously.

"I'm on horseback behind three medieval knights," she narrated "They're called Bors, Percival and Galahad - I know that cause they have names stencilled on the back of their armour, just like the players in the soccer cup final I was watching last night. So that's handy."

Jensen ground his teeth.

"It's dark. It's night. They're approaching an old, ruined castle, though there's a light coming from one of the windows. Percival is eating a chicken leg and it's pissing the other two off cause he keeps wiping his hands on their mount's caparisons. Bors has gotten really narked and threatened to stick his mace right up Percival's culet, whatever that is…"

"Too descriptive!" Jensen snapped at the glass, though it was obvious Edith couldn't hear him.

"How does this set-up work, then?" Murphy tried again.

"The computer… it's a quantum computer. It can calculate infinite possibilities. See?"

Murphy didn't see.

"Well," Jenson continued. "They say that, if you think you understand quantum physics, you don't understand quantum physics. So it's hard to explain."

"Try."

"OK. Eh… We can use the computer to break down all matter into its basic components and study their trajectories." The scientist traced the imaginary fragments with his fingers, looking a bit like the world's palest rapper. "How they move, you know? Where they go. And... once you know how something moves and where it goes, you can tell where it once... was. Our quantum computer does that, yes."

"Quite a feat."

"It's a big computer." Jensen was still watching Edith, who had begun speaking again.

"Percival is bursting for the toilet but it takes forever to unfasten all those straps. And Bors is still in a monumental huff, so Galahad is going in alone. I'm following him. There's a strong smell of sulphur. He's entering a little room and there's a really old bloke there, sitting by a fire. He looks a bit like Sean Connery. For some reason, he's surrounded by old-fashioned goblets. A couple of them seem to be solid gold and some are crusted with jewels."

The woman pulled a wad of gum from her mouth and stuck it under the console. She suddenly sounded a lot clearer.

"He's asking Galahad to pick which relic he thinks is the Holy Grail. Holy shit! Says if he gets it wrong, he'll die. That's a hell of a risk just to get a cuppa."

"This is an awful lot like the plot of *Indiana Jones and the Last Crusade*," Murphy said suspiciously.

"She watches a lot of TV." Jensen raised his bony shoulders in resignation. "What can you do?"

"Then why are you using her?" Murphy picked at a smear on the pane.

"Ah. That's the tricky part." Jenson stroked his chin. "As I said, the quantum computer analyses the trajectories of every bit of material in the world and then projects backwards. And so... we can chart exactly where each particle was located at any given moment... right back to the dawn of time, if you like."

"That's amazing." Murphy gave a low whistle. "The possibilities must be endless."

"Actually, we haven't found a useful application for it at all," Jensen admitted. "We can't even make a bomb. Ce'st la vie, I suppose. Scientists are a bit like explorers. Some find America. Some discover Lapland."

"And?"

"And what?"

"Who discovered Lapland?"

"Beats me." The scientist glanced sideways at Murphy to gauge if his interest was genuine. "If you really want to know, we can find out."

He pointed into the booth.

"See, that's what Sonja there does. Builds up a complete map of the past. She can *see* history."

"Sonja, does all that?" Murphy looked at the woman with new admiration. "So, why does her badge say Edith?"

"Sonja's the name of the computer," Jensen replied scathingly. "Edith is a religious nutter. But... if she can discover something valuable, like the final resting place of the Grail or... a bit of the true cross? Well...

that would give us the money to keep running for years."

Edith began speaking again.

"Galahad is having a good look at all the different cups. He's hovering over the really fancy ones. Not surprising, really. They must be worth a fortune.

"This is our real stumbling block," Jensen whispered, so as not to drown out the woman's commentary. "In order to properly monitor history, our *Witnesses*, as we call them, need to hook themselves directly into the quantum computer. They have a symbiotic relationship, you might call it. They link together. Yes. Fuse."

"Isn't that a bit dangerous?" Murphy looked at the wires protruding from Edith's head and gave a shudder.

"That's why we use people like her."

"You don't like women much, do you?"

"I love women," Jensen snapped. "I just don't like Edith."

"Still…. this is fantastic." Murphy wasn't about to get in the middle of a personality clash. "You could learn so much about… Everything."

"That was the idea, yes," Jensen agreed. "But like every new project, it has a few… em… glitches."

"The wrinkly dude is reminding him that the Grail was used by Our Lord at the last supper." Edith carried on, oblivious at being the focus of attention. Murphy assumed the window only worked one way.

"Hey, you old fucker! Stop helping him out. No cheating!" She snapped her fingers indignantly. "Now Galahad's studying the plain wooden ones. That seems a better bet, but I'm still not sure it's right."

"See, it's like she's actually there," Jensen hissed behind his hand.

"Glitches?" Murphy asked.

"Sort of." His companion grimaced. "According to Edith, when Judas kissed Jesus in the Garden of Gethsemane, Christ punched him in the mouth."

He snorted his disapproval.

"How do you think a revelation like that would go down with the Christian community?"

"No shit!" Murphy gave a gasp. "That really happened?"

"But Galahad's no dummy. He's put the wooden goblet down and is still considering. That's it. Left a bit. Warmer. Warmer. Red hot!"

Edith gave a smug smile and punched the air.

"Yes! He's gone for the ceramic mug with *What Would Jesus Do?* written on it."

Her face had taken on a faraway look.

"Isn't that funny? I've got one just like it at home."

"Who knows?" Jensen scowled at the woman. "That's problem number two. The Witness becomes... eh... *part* of any given scene they observe. Their emotional state and desires influences their... interpretation, if you like."

He gave a stoic shrug.

"Now we have to employ a team of psychologists to separate what really happened from what the Witness wants to happen. It's costing us a fortune."

"So, where do I come in?" Murphy had a cold feeling in the pit of his stomach.

"You kidding?" Jensen opened the clipboard and began to read the contents. "Billy Wayne Murphy. Life imprisonment for the murder of two eleven-year-old girls. Psychologists say you've never shown remorse. Have no emotional involvement with what you've done. In any capacity whatsoever."

He raised an inquisitive eyebrow.

"I can't imagine how that must feel. Which is the whole point, really."

"It doesn't feel like anything at all," Murphy said coldly.

"Of course. Of course." The scientist shut the clipboard with a snap. Ofcoureseofcourseofcourse."

"Because I'm innocent, you idiot," Murphy fumed. "I was framed."

"A man without emotions." Jensen was still lost in his own musings. "Absolutely perfect. You'll be able to trawl through history in an objective manner. Aha. See things exactly as they are. You're just what we need to save the project."

"I am *not* a psychopath," Murphy repeated. "I was fixing my toilet at the time."

An incredible thought struck him.

"Listen!" he said excitedly. "We could use your machine to prove my innocence! Go back and find who actually killed those girls!"

He tried to grab hold of the scientist's arm but both hands were shackled to his legs by chains.

"We already did." Jensen glared at him and pulled away. "It was definitely you."

"Wait a bloody minute!" Murphy exploded. "You just said if the observer expects me to be the killer, or *wants* it to be me, then that's exactly what they'll see. Right?"

"Correct." Jensen nodded happily in agreement.

"So, who was the sodding witness?"

"Me."

"You bastard!" Murphy tried to lunge at the scientist but his chains snapped tight and he fell flat on his face.

"You're hardly going to be impartial yourself, eh?" Jensen bent down and pulled the fallen man to his feet. "At least helping us gets you out of prison."

Murphy thought for a while. A slow smile spread across his face.

"When you plug *me* into Sonja, I could see who really committed the crime." His eyes sparkled with hope. "Once we know, we might be able to find physical evidence to back that up."

"Ehm…" Jensen looked sheepish. "Not anymore,"

"S'cuse me?"

"It's a quantum thing. Schrödinger's Cat and all that stuff." The scientist pursed his lips. "Once a past event has been observed on a quantum level, it kind of... *becomes* history. To all intents and purposes."

Murphy's brow furrowed.

"Take your case, for instance," Jensen continued. "Did you kill those kids? There are only two possibilities: yes or no. But... ehhh... now that I've looked at it, there's only one. You definitely did it."

He spread his hands generously.

"Therefore, you may as well assist us. Get off death row, eh?"

"I'm *not* a psychopath," Murphy shouted. "I *have* emotions. My view of history won't be worth a crap."

"Shhhhh! Nobody has to know that." Jensen put an urgent finger to his lips. "We need you on board to keep up corporate funding. The Chairman's patience is running out."

"Oh. I see. Right." Murphy's face was like thunder. "Well, since the morality of this project also seems to be a thing of the past, why don't you just pretend Sonja found some terrible scandal in this... Chairman's past and blackmail him into keeping it going?"

"Because we needed a totally credible witness to take on someone *that* powerful," Jensen smirked. "Which is where you come in."

"And people call *me* criminally insane." Murphy snarled.

"Yes. Well. You don't have to be mad to work here, but it helps." Jensen's smile widened into a manic grin. "Ha hah. Hahahahahahahahahahahahahaha. Sorry."

He pointed to a door behind them.

"The guards will take you for briefing and inductance now. We'll expect you online in a couple of days."

Murphy's shoulders drooped and the chains clinked sadly.

"Maybe you're right," he said finally.

"Good man." Jensen patted him gingerly on the shoulder.

"I mean, you've proved I'm a stone-cold killer, then double-crossed me, eh?" Murphy gave a warped grin. "So, *your* days are most definitely numbered."

"Statements like that aren't going to go down well with your parole officer," Jensen blanched.

"Just watch your back, that's all." Murphy turned and shuffled his way out of the door, the scientist following a safe distance behind.

Edith waited until the men were gone. She punched a few buttons on her console, inserted an earpiece and began to talk into the microphone again.

"Chairman? It's me. Just went back and looked into the past, as ordered. Your suspicions are confirmed. Professor Jensen was obsessed with the impending failure of his project and intended to blackmail you for some fabricated indiscretion to keep his funding coming."

She adjusted her wig.

"He enlisted a psychopathic convict called Murphy to facilitate his scheme, but the potential Witness threatened to kill him. Since the professor was found dead a few days later, I assume Murphy found a way to make good his promise."

She coughed politely.

"If you like, I can look at the day Professor Jensen died, just to be sure. No? Oh. You've already done that. I understand... Absolutely, Chairman."

She nodded sagely.

"Let sleeping dogs lie, eh? Or else they might come back and bite you on the arse." She glanced at her watch. "In that case, I've a couple of hours before lunch."

Edith switched off the microphone. She retrieved her gum from under the console, popped it back in her mouth and sat back contentedly.

"Just enough time to find out what happened to a certain 30 pieces of silver."

Moving in a Mysterious Way

People are being exposed to a daily cocktail of pollution that may be having a significant impact on their health.

BBC News

I survived the apocalypse cause I was in Sunnyvale prison canteen, waiting to visit my cousin Dave. I didn't want to talk to the other sad sacks, so I put on wraparound sunglasses and noise-cancelling headphones.

That's what saved my life.

Nobody knows what happened to the air. All we're sure about is that human beings suffered an instant and complete sensory overload.

Suddenly, sunlight blinded people and burned their skin to a crisp. Every noise was amplified to a deafening roar. Each smell, sweet or sour, became an overpowering stench.

The end of the world came with a whimper that felt like a bang.

Out of nowhere, the prison sirens went off. Sirens are loud by definition but this was in a different league.

Everyone started screaming, not the wisest course of action when you're caught up in a maelstrom of unbearable sound. Through a porthole in the door, I could see a stampede for the exits, including guys in leg irons, who had to hop. Light pouring through the upper windows turned swiftly and intolerably bright, as if an enormous sun lamp had been switched on.

I threaded my way between visitors, bumping into each other in panic, eyes squeezed shut and hands over their ears. My head was splitting, despite the headphones, so I darted into the kitchen, holding my nose. Prison food smells awful at the best of times but now the stink was stomach-churning. There was a big walk-in fridge at the back, so I got inside and pulled the door shut. Then I ate a thawing sausage roll and waited in the dark until blessed silence descended.

When I emerged, it was night and the place was deserted. No visitors. No warders. No prisoners. No Dave.

I presume one of the guards opened the electronic cell doors, as a last act of altruism, setting the inmates free. Or, maybe he just pressed the wrong button in confusion. Either way, I doubt anyone made it more than a hundred yards outside the main gate before they got toasted.

Everything happens for a reason, mum used to say. Then again, she was electrocuted by faulty Christmas tree lights and was obviously no expert on fate.

Everyone has different theories but shit happens and I don't see the point in dwelling on it. After all, the Bible has God creating the whole universe in seven days without actually saying how he did it. And the whole shebang only takes up half a page.

But I've always been lucky and it turned out jail was the best place for me - which is something else my mum used to say. Sunnyvale's male and female wings were subterranean, joined by underground tunnels, while metal shutters could be brought down on any windows above ground. The place even had its own emergency generator and I'd say the end of humanity definitely counted as an emergency.

For a while, I thought I might be the last person on earth. Then, one by one, I came across Corrine Telford, Floyd Peterson, WTF Hartley, Div and Doob. I still don't know Div and Doob's last names. Or their first names, for that matter. There's no real need to inquire when your universe only contains six people.

We get along well enough. Each of us has staked out a little bit of turf but everyone chips in to keep things running. Like vampires, we only come out at night and there are solitary confinement cells on the lowest levels, where we can sleep the day away without being assaulted by sounds, smells and piercing light.

All in all, it's not a bad existence, considering the circumstances.

As I said, I've always been lucky.

WTF Hartley and I are a couple. He isn't really called WTF, of course, but now he can have any handle he wants. Personally, I would have gone for something like Dirk Manly or Rupert Hyphen Poshhouser. Still, it kind of suits him.

He also wears a dress most days. Not in a feminine way, because he has a shaved head and a face that looks like it vacuumed a gravel driveway. WTF just doesn't see any reason to conform to old stereotypes. Then again, he has a broad Scottish accent, so perhaps it's the closest thing he can find to a kilt.

He also has the most important and hazardous job in Sunnyvale, foraging for supplies in town once a week.

We've developed a routine. I lather his face with sun cream while he distracts us both from the dangers he faces with a stream of meaningless banter. He keeps his voice low, as everyone does, so it's no more than a murmur. I don't mind, as it sounds quite sexy.

"I ever tell you about going tae the wildlife sanctuary in Lone Pine?" he says. "I had mah picture taken with a Koala called Monica. Grabbed mah bare arms with claws that could open a safe door, then peed on me. Close up, I saw she had beady eyes and wuz incapable of any kind of expression. Like a psychopath."

He puts on several prison uniforms, each bigger than the last. It's fortunate some of the inmates were built like garden sheds.

"In the gift shop were photographs of famous people holding Koalas. President Clinton. Pope John Paul II. Even Bono. If aliens landed, they'd probably think Monica wuz some kind of world leader."

He sticks on a riot helmet, skiing goggles, rubber gloves, earplugs and nose plugs.

"Koalas. The wee bastards hae everybody fooled."

I help him into a leather flying jacket and white silk scarf he found in a vintage store. He likes to be stylish. I unbent a wire coat hanger and threaded it through the collar of the jacket, so now it stands up and protects his neck. It looks pretty cool too. Being civilized is all about keeping up appearances, WTF insists, and I agree.

"You take care out there," I warn, as always.

"I am putting myself to the fullest possible use, which is all I think that any conscious entity can ever hope to do." He gives me a thumbs up. "That's the killer computer HAL, from the movie *2001*. Douglas Rain did the voice."

WTF is a film buff.

I gently slap his butt and retreat while he opens the door to the compound. In the distance, I can see silhouettes of redundant guard towers. Even with nose plugs in, I get a whiff of a thousand odours, sharp as Gorgonzola. Thank goodness the sun has turned the corpses to dust, or we'd be eternally throwing up.

WTF blows me a kiss, steps into the night and is gone.

Time to do my rounds.

I'm officially head of security, prison nurse, health inspector and entertainment officer. Always liked to keep busy. I'm also Mayor of Brisbane and Duchess of Queensland, though those are honorary titles. I've pushed to be addressed as Queen of Royal Britain Land and Its Associated Colonies but nobody has taken me up on it.

First stop on my route is Corinne Telford.

Corinne is our cook, garbage collector and spiritual adviser. She's also a born again Christian and thinks what happened is God's punishment on the wicked - which completely fails to explain anything. Whatever floats your boat, I suppose.

Corrine survived by hiding inside an empty coffin in the prison chapel and, out of gratitude, made it her domain. It once had beautiful stained-glass windows, telling the story of Christ rising from his tomb and suchlike, but we've boarded them over. Now they're hidden behind cheap plywood facades, which would probably make a good parable, if I could be bothered thinking one up.

Corinne spends most of her time reading the Bible and waiting in vain for the rest of us to come seeking guidance. I suggested she become a Jehovah's Witness so she could be more proactive and knock on doors. We can't exactly pretend we're not at home. She called me an unholy blasphemer, so I added that to my list of titles.

And she's obviously not too dogmatic, as she followed my advice. Sure enough, everyone claimed to be out.

Since none of us have rushed to be converted, I like to keep Corinne's holy spirits up. Each day, I present her with a theological question to ponder, hoping for a satisfying discussion.

"How's trick's, Coz?" I stick my head around the door.

"Please do come in. Mo." She beckons to me. "Would you like an Anzac biscuit?"

I accept and sit on a pew. I imagine it's a bit like communion, not that I've ever been to one.

"Right, Corrine." I launch straight in, as she isn't the type for idle chit-chat. "God is supposed to be all-powerful, yeah?"

"That is what I believe, Mo. Certainly."

Corinne has taken to speaking in a formal manner she probably considers saintly. It actually makes her sound a bit like HAL, which WTF finds hilarious. I don't know why she doesn't go the whole hog and throw in a few 'thous' and 'beholds'.

"Then here's my question, Coz. Is God able to build a wall so high, he can't jump over it?"

"Yes." No hesitation there.

"But if he can't jump over it, he's not all-powerful, is he?"

"He moves in mysterious ways, Mo."

"There's nothing very mysterious about jumping."

"It is not for me to question the Lord," she replies serenely. "We are simply here to serve."

I bristle a little at this. As far as I'm concerned, the only people put on earth to serve are waiters. But I know she'll think about it. Maybe pause before that wall she's building around herself gets too high to jump over.

"You remembering tomorrow is the big night?" I cajole. "You gotta do something for it."

As entertainment officer, I have organised a talent show. In case that isn't enough of a challenge, I've given it a theme. Air.

Why not? I think it's funny and so does WTF.

"I have cleared my calendar." Corinne licks crumbs from her fingers and I wonder if she just made a joke. "I shall be there, never fear."

"You're not going to give a sermon, are you?" I wince.

"Everyone has their own area of expertise," she replies haughtily. "It would be foolish not to use mine."

"Of course." I try to sound enthusiastic. "Looking forward to it."

I back out the door, crouched low and waving both hands in front of my face. Corrine looks suitably puzzled.

"What on earth are you doing?"

"God's not the only one who can move in a mysterious way."

Corrine sighs.

Next stop is Floyd Peterson. As always, he's in the prison education centre, lost in thought. On the wall is a whiteboard where some unknown dead guy has written *You can't buy happiness, so steal it,* along with a drawing of a crab on a bike. Try as I might, I can't get the connection.

"Evening, professor."

He appreciates it when I call him professor. In the old days, he was a prison janitor, saved by being in the lowest level, cleaning toilets when real shit hit the fan. He thinks our predicament is the result of mass quantum entanglement set off by particle smashing in Switzerland.

I sit at a desk near the back of the room, like a naughty pupil, while he stands at the front.

Floyd Peterson tilts his head down whenever he looks at me. He must have worn glasses once, but nobody needs them anymore, as our sight is crystal clear. The rest of us often sport sunshades but I guess he was pretty myopic and relishes having 20/20 vision.

I think I understand why people lose their eyesight as they age. When they study themselves in the mirror, they're pleasantly blurred and it hides the wrinkles. That's why, the older you get, the less inclined you are to have photographs taken. Nobody wants a portrait of their own Dorian Gray.

It makes me appreciate WTF even more. Though I'm getting on in years, he looks at me as if I'm the last ham sandwich at a weight watchers convention. Which, in metaphorical terms, I suppose I am.

"Whatcha pondering today, Prof?" I inquire.

"I was thinking that there are billions of stars and planets out there." He points in the direction of the roof. It is a mass of white splodges made by bored inmates chewing paper and throwing them upwards till they stick. It reminds me of the night sky but I don't think he's ever noticed.

Floyd Peterson is determined to live in his own head.

"In the good old days, we were unable to reach any of those myriad wonders. Didn't bother us in the slightest, did it?"

To be honest, it always did, but I let the comment slide.

"Ever been to Venice?" he continues. "Or Amsterdam? Moscow? Krakow? Munich? Edinburgh? Tokyo? Rhodes? Chicago?"

"I went to Bundaberg once," I venture. "But it was Sunday, so everything was shut."

"All those fine places," he says wistfully. "Yet, when we had the opportunity to visit them, we never took it."

He spreads his hands.

"Why should we care now that we can't?"

Actually, I *have* been to most of those places, Venice being my favourite. But that doesn't fit with his theory either, so I stay mum.

"It's simply a process of adjustment. See, all experience is filtered through the prism of our own perceptions and feelings, so it doesn't really matter where we are."

"The prison of our own perceptions and feelings?" I raise an eyebrow.

Floyd Peterson stares at me and I instinctively put a hand to my face. These days, if I've got a bit of food on my chin, it can most likely be spotted from another planet.

"Prism, Mo," he scolds. "Don't take the piss."

"Sorry." But I still think my interpretation is more accurate.

"Thanks for the lecture, Prof." I get up, careful not to scrape my chair on the tile floor. The noise would be teeth-jarring. "You always give me a lot to think about."

Mostly, I am thinking Floyd Peterson needs a hobby. Live in your own head long enough and you stop being comfortable anywhere else.

"Ready for tomorrow night?" I change the subject. "The big show?"

"Not really. But I'll give it a try."

Next on my rounds are Div and Doob, who live in the gymnasium. They're our mechanical wizards, keeping the generator and other gee-gaws running. They were sleeping off massive hangovers in a disused lead boiler when Armageddon came along and, most likely, didn't notice. Their theory is some big conglomerate invented a formula to remove pollutants choking our atmosphere and it got out of control.

Both are in their early twenties and I suspect they're in love because the rest of us are too old to be of consequence. They quite like me, though. Most people do.

I believe they're suffering from SMWD or Social Media Withdrawal Symptom, a condition I completely made up but sounds about right. They've even created a homemade Facebook page, writing post-it notes and sticking them to the wall. Visitors can tick the ones they like with a red pen on a string.

When I slide in, they are opening a box of wine.

"G'day, mates." I plonk myself between them and give both a peck on the cheek. Even that small gesture tingles as if I've rubbed my lips along sandpaper.

"Hi, Mo." Div passes me a drink. "Heard you coming, so we broke out the best glasses. The foggy ones with decorative soap rings."

I take a slurp. It's like swallowing turpentine in this new atmosphere, but all booze tastes horrible until you get used to it. Ask any teenager.

"Hope you've been practising your act," I splutter, trying not to cough.

Div and Doob regard my talent show as akin to a Victorian get-together, singing psalms around the pianoforte. But they're also bored out of their minds and welcome any distraction.

"Don't you know it!" They grin at each other. "We're gonna win for sure."

"There are no winners or losers, you know."

"Spoken like a true loser. We demand a prize."

"I'll see what I can do."

We shoot the breeze for a while and drink more wine, grimacing with each sip, until it's time for WTF to return. Then I make my excuses and leave.

I help WTF out of his clothes and he goes for a shower, which takes a long time. Anything more than a trickle of lukewarm water is painful. In the meantime, I take out the contents of his rucksack which, as usual, consists mostly of tinned food.

"Baked beans," I say brightly. "There's a surprise."

"Aye, but these are low sodium."

There are also two bottles of port, some cheese crackers and six pairs of oven gloves.

I look quizzically at him but he just taps his long nose.

I found WTF sitting calmly in a padded solitary confinement cell, with the door unlocked but closed. The only inmate smart enough not to make a run for it.

I don't know what he did and I've never queried him about it. I'm not a curious type, nor one for emotional sandblasting. We've all been given a second chance and he has made the most of his. I wish there was a parole board around to witness it.

WTF's theory is that the air is exactly the same as always - it's us who have suddenly become intolerant to it. He says it's proof people can change.

"Want me to make you dinner?" I ask. This is our little joke, as heating food would require an asbestos suit. We have to eat everything cold.

"When I originally came here," WTF talks carefully over the noise of the water. "I went tae a restaurant in Apollo Bay and ordered my first proper Aussie burger."

He turns off the faucet and I hand him a towel.

"It took three members of staff to lift onto the table. It had lettuce, tomato, pineapple, a fried egg, watercress, bacon, some kind of hairy plant I didn't recognise but might be cactus, a cigarette butt, ketchup, mayo, more pineapple, cotton, ice cream and a Bush Turkey sitting on top, in case I couldnae finish it. There may have been meat in there as well, but I gave up the will tae live halfway through and had to be rolled back to mah car."

He chuckles roguishly. But his eyes are sunken and his skin is puckered like a prune.

"How come you guys put pineapple on everything?"

That's why I like WTF. He makes me laugh. Or he tries, which is just as good.

"You go to your cell and get some rest," I command sternly. "Those trips outside are taking a real toll."

"I've seen things you people wouldn't believe," he quotes. "That's Rutger Hauer as the killer replicant Roy Batty in *Blade Runner*."

"Let me put everything away." I hang up the towel. "Need you on top form for tomorrow night, baby."

"I won't let you down." He smiles resignedly and plods off.

Though we are lovers, I don't sleep with WTF. The touch of flesh on flesh is too extreme to stand in more than small bursts. And if one of us started snoring, it would end in fisticuffs.

Instead, I go to my own cell, take a bottle of wine and a strip of Diazepam from under the mattress and down both.

We each cope in our way. This has always been mine.

The next night, everyone files into the prison hall and sits in the back row. They are certainly dressed for the occasion, sporting finery WTF brought back from his last trip to the mall. Corrine has on a full-length fur coat. Floyd Peterson is in a dinner suit and bow tie. Div and Doob have on pork pie hats and striped braces over white T-shirts. WTF is resplendent in a red mini skirt and silver spangled halter top. He hands each of us a pair of oven gloves and I finally understand.

It's so we can clap without making too much noise.

The stage is basic, just a raised wooden platform with one metal flagpole at either side, minus the flag.

Not exactly the Sydney Opera House, but it'll have to suffice. I appear from the rear door, clutching a sheaf of computer paper.

"Good evening, ladies and gentlemen," I announce softly. "And welcome to the first annual Sunnyvale talent contest. I've prepared a small speech for the occasion."

I let the perforated paper unfurl and spill across the boards for several feet. The audience gives a stifled moan.

"Tough crowd, eh? In that case, without further ado, let me introduce Div and Doob - the gruesome twosome."

Div and Doob spring up and move along the line of bemused participants, shaking hands and patting them gently on the shoulders. Then they scramble onto the stage and stand at opposite ends.

"Check this out," Div chuckles. "I will now make some shit appear from thin... air."

Going with the theme. Well done, Div.

He runs one hand up his leg and produces a large piece of dried fruit, seemingly from nowhere. On his wrist is a small gold timepiece that wasn't there before.

"Hey! That's my snack," Floyd Peterson frowns. "It was in my pocket."

"And he's wearing my watch," Corinne adds. "I shall be wanting that back, young man."

Div puts the fruit on his head and stands perfectly still.

"Oooh, what a lovely pear," Doob says appreciatively.

"You took the words right out of my mouth," Div shoots back and the audience groans again. They *are* a tough crowd.

"That's fae the movie *Carry on Doctor*," WTF stage whispers. "Stop nicking jokes, you wee shits."

Doob pulls a knife from her sleeve, twirls it around her fingers and grins at him. WTF pats his top, suitably impressed.

"You've got mah shiv," he whistles appreciatively. "Well played, lassie."

Before anyone can object, Doob tosses it in the air, catches the blade and throws. It shoots across the stage, imbeds itself in the pear and tumbles into the wings.

Every jaw is open. Div and Doob take this as a positive sign, mime high-fiving each other and return to their seats. I begin to suspect they might not have been part of the maintenance crew after all. But the show must go on.

"Next up is that master of mirth and purveyor of puns, WTF Hartley." I beckon to my partner, expecting him to do some sort of stand-up routine. Instead, he grabs a basket from his feet, bounces up the steps and opens it.

It is filled with balloons, long thin and multicoloured.

He blows them up, turning bright red in the process and everyone grabs their earplugs. One pop will send us into a coma. But he begins to fold them expertly into each other. They have been lubricated with cooking spray so the rubber won't squeak - we can smell it, even at a distance. Within a few seconds, a sculpture begins to take shape, a donkey or perhaps an alligator. Either way, I'm impressed he's made an effort to stick with the subject matter. I should have known he'd try hard to please.

He lets go and the animal whizzes over our head, deflating as it twists, producing a seemingly endless wet fart. In the amplified atmosphere, the sound is exaggeratedly comical.

Everyone starts giggling.

"Thank you. I'll be here all week. Probably all year." WTF holds up a trembling hand. "Try the veal."

He glances nervously at me as I regain the podium and my heart goes out to him.

"And now, Professor Floyd Peterson," I say. "No idea what he's going to do but it's bound to be intellectual. Take it away, Prof."

Floyd Peterson brings his folding chair to the stage and sits on it. Takes a homemade carved recorder from his jacket. He puts the instrument to his lips and blows as softly as he can. It is *The Lark Ascending* by Vaughn Williams.

He plays it perfectly.

The thin, reedy tune floats around us and up into the rafters. One by one, we remove our earplugs.

Amplified by the clear air, the sound becomes as full-bodied and moving as any orchestra.

We are rapt. From my position in the wings, I can see tears running down upturned faces. Floyd Peterson finishes and we wait until the last echoes have died away before clapping. He smiles gratefully and returns with his seat.

I wish I hadn't decided to let Corrine go last. Unless she can turn water into wine, she'll ruin the moment for sure. Unfortunately, it's too late now.

"Finally, we welcome Corrine Telford." I try my best to sound keen. "Who, I'm certain, is going to give us all something divine."

Corrine makes her way hesitantly into the limelight. She takes a deep breath and I wait for her to launch into some diatribe about the glory of God.

Instead, she unfastens her fur coat and lets it fall. Underneath, she is wearing nothing but a silver, two-piece bathing costume. Her body is lean and muscular, the kind of physique you only get after years of push-ups and crunches.

What the hell?

Corrine grabs one of the metal poles at the side of the stage and effortlessly flips upside down. Begins to slowly revolve, her long blonde hair brushing the floor.

The silence is palpable.

She lets go with one hand and curls into the pole, spinning faster. What the sensation of cold metal is doing to her skin, I can't imagine, but it makes my toes curl.

The audience's eyes are on stalks.

There's no way she can pull off what I think is coming next. Yet she does.

Corrine removes her other hand and draws up her knees, holding on with only her stomach muscles. I put a hand to my mouth and the others give a collective intake of breath.

Eventually, Corrine slows to a stop and pirouettes back onto the stage as casually as if she were dismounting a bike. Her face is flushed but she is barely out of breath.

"There's moving in a fucking mysterious way for you, Mo," she hisses.

The applause is thunderous. Or it would have been if we weren't wearing oven gloves.

"That is bloody art, so it is!" Div removes his hat and salutes. "Respect, woman."

Corrine puts her coat back on, comes down and sits next to Floyd Peterson. She is shivering, so he puts his arm around her and she nestles into his shoulder.

This certainly is a night for surprises.

"I want to thank you all from the bottom of my heart." I wrap things up with a curtsey. "There's port and nibbles in the foyer. Well... that table at the back."

My voice is choked with emotion.

"Tonight has been such a success that, next year, we're putting on a musical."

"I vote for *Godspell*," Corrine says. All of us laugh, loudly as we dare.

The cast party is a happy affair. We are all a bit in awe of each other and there is a sense of camaraderie that wasn't there before. Each of us knows it takes a long time to perfect tricks like these, not just a few days.

More like years surviving on the streets than rotting in a cell.

For the first time, they begin to talk about the future. Floyd Peterson floats the idea of irrigating our prison yard and planting vegetables under a homemade sail. Corinne offers to help, admitting she grew up on a farm. Div and Doob casually mention they used to grow marijuana and know a lot about fertiliser.

When the rest have retired, WTF takes me onto the roof because that's our place. The sky is damp with glittering stars and the world is mostly silent. Occasionally, we hear the chirp of an insect far in the distance.

"Not everything is dead after all." I cup my ear. "There might even be other people out there."

"Life, uh, finds a way." WTF does a passable American accent. "That's Jeff Goldblum in *Jurassic Park*."

He opens a tin of peaches and the bottle of port he saved for us.

"I think you'll find this a cheeky wee number," he deadpans. "It has overpowering notes of barbecue sauce and a kick like a prostitute with epilepsy."

I take a sip and wrinkle my nose.

"Well done tonight, Mo." He hands me the can. "But I was looking forward tae your effort. How come ye didnae do something?"

"I was the compere. Wouldn't have felt right, joining in."

We each try to eat a slice of fruit, but the taste is so strong and sweet that it stings our mouths. We spit them out, smirk at each other and I wait for him to launch into one of his funny stories.

Instead, WTF gazes out over the vista.

"Look at this view," he remarks. "It's beautiful but kind of sad and empty."

He glances sideways at me.

"When I was younger, I used tae think the right person for me wuz someone who'd sit by my side and feel exactly the way I did about a scene like this."

He frames me in a little box shaped by his fingers.

"But no. The right person is really someone who fits *intae* that picture."

He sighs and it reverberates loudly over the roof. The sound is unexpectedly heartbreaking.

"Thing is, just cause someone is perfect for one scene, it doesnae mean they'll be right for the next, eh?"

I've underestimated WTF Hartley.

"Why exactly did you come to Australia?" I break my rule and finally ask him a question.

"Land built by convicts, eh?" he yuks. "Maybe I thought I'd fit intae *that* picture."

"I love you WTF." I stroke his cheek.

"I love you too." He tries to stifle a yawn. "Why don't you come downstairs?

"I told Div and Doob the show wasn't a competition. Didn't say there weren't prizes. I want to leave them out while everyone is asleep."

"You are most definitely the bee's knees." He clasps his hands together in an imitation of the scene from the film he's quoting.

"Andy Garcia." I pick up the thread. "The killer turned hero from *Things to Do In Denver When You're Dead*."

"Clever lassie. What am *I* getting, then?"

"Stay awake long enough?" I nudge him. "You'll find out."

"There's no way I'm nodding off now."

He kisses the top of my head and leaves with a spring in his step.

I sit for a long time, wrapped in soft-skinned silence. Then I go downstairs, unlock the storage cupboard of level three and retrieve a stash of goodies.

Time to make my rounds.

I raided the prison library for the Quaran, the Tripitakas and the Torah, which I stack outside the chapel door. Corinne may as well keep her options open.

Next, I go to the education centre and set down a telescope I took from the guard tower. Floyd Peterson can use it to look at the stars, though he'll finally have to put sunglasses on. It won't bring them any closer but it might seem like they are.

For Div and Doob, I leave a couple of hazmat suits, which took me ages to find. They were once used for scrubbing cells, when inmates smeared faecal matter on the walls. Floyd Person would have known they existed if he really had been a janitor.

WTF has done enough. It's time Div and Doob started putting their light-fingered talents to better use. Anyway, they need to get out more.

Then I enter WTF's cell and take off my clothes.

We have sex quietly and gently because there's no other way to do it. It's very intense and also rather uncomfortable. Forced intimacy turning something that used to be fun into a bit of a chore.

Afterwards, we lie, side by side, fingers entwined. It's all we can manage.

"You're the glue that keeps this lot together, Mo. Know that?" Though it is dark, I can see WTF has on a serious face. "You've turned us intae a family."

"Like the mafia?"

"Nah. I mean it."

He closes his eyes and I wait until his breathing is deep and regular before getting dressed. Wisps of my white hair remain on the pillow.

I spot the basket in the corner and sigh. Making balloon animals is not something you learn in jail. More like the props a failed entertainer would use if he was performing for a bunch of convicts.

It's nice to know we have something in common.

"You don't have to pretend anymore." I softly kiss his cheek. "You're one of them."

Me? I had a family once and sure as hell don't need another. I was bored enough with my last life. Besides, I've used up all the pills in the pharmacy, WTF has emptied the local bottle shop of wine and I can't stand spirits.

WTF will understand, I hope. He knows how exhausting it is, pretending to fit in.

I go upstairs and struggle into the prison outfits. Stick on the riot helmet and glasses. Insert the nose and earplugs. Take the leather flying jacket and white silk scarf from a coat hanger and wrap them around myself. They smell strongly of WTF and, I imagine, always will. But, unlike him, my armour is for defence - not crusading.

Everyone will have their theory as to why I left. In the end, I put on a great show, though. That's what they'll remember.

I edge open the gates and step outside. I was hoping for a sense of freedom but, inside this getup, everything is muffled and dark.

I'll travel by night and hide in cellars during the day, though the air could still get me in some un-guarded moment. I console myself by imagining, for a fleeting second, it might feel like being born again.

I'd love to go to Venice, as I could afford to live there now, but Sydney will have to do. I'll move into a suite on the top floor of the Waldorf Astoria with a balcony overlooking the opera house. Watch the stars, drink champagne and dine on tinned caviar, even if it tastes like crap.

There won't be anyone to share the view or feel the way I do about it, but I'm used to that. I'll survive, as usual.

To be honest, the end of the world hasn't really made much difference to me.

As I say, I've always been lucky.

ABOUT THE AUTHOR

Jan-Andrew Henderson (J.A. Henderson) is the author of 40 teenage, YA, adult and non-fiction books. Published in the UK, USA, Australia, Canada and Europe, he has been shortlisted for sixteen literary awards and is the winner of the Aurealis Award, the Doncaster Book Prize and the Royal Mail Award.

www.janandrewhenderson.com